Forever Not Measured

Forever Not Measured

Graeme van der Meer

She who wandered. And found me.

CONTENTS

One

Signal Loss

Mira Grant stood at the helm of Siren, a 28-foot Hallberg-Rassy yacht that had been her grandfather's pride. He had always wanted her to return to Greece, and Siren, passed down to her after his passing, made sure of this. Mira felt the cruiser cut through the water with just the gentle hum of the wind and the soft creak of the lines as the sails caught the breeze. It was a quiet boat, perfect for her—a vessel built for solitude, not show. The teak deck, worn smooth by years of salt and sun, felt like an extension of herself, grounded and steady.

The Mediterranean Sea stretched before her, its blue expanse glittering beneath the late afternoon sun. In the distance, the Ionian Islands lay bathed in soft golden light, their rocky cliffs rising sharply from the water. Mira adjusted the wheel, letting the boat glide across the water with a confidence that was second nature to her.

James, lounging lazily in the cockpit, was a distraction. He was tan, handsome, and profoundly unmoored from anything resembling purpose. He'd come from money—old money, big houses and private tutors. He'd never held a real job, never needed to. The kind of man who could float through life on charm and access. He wasn't a bad guy, just... a project. The kind of man she was always fixing before they found their forever home—if they ever did.

"You should slow down," James called out, barely looking up from his phone. "Enjoy the view. We've got time."

Mira didn't respond right away, but she caught herself sighing inwardly. She adjusted the sails again, steering Siren on a southward course toward Paxos, about an hour away. She'd always enjoyed this part of the journey—the island's charming villages and peaceful coastline. It was the kind of place that felt timeless, a reminder of simpler days. Gaios, the main village, nestled along the shore, was small enough to feel intimate yet large enough to find a quiet corner for reflection.

She let the yacht continue at its own pace, knowing exactly how much wind to catch. The familiar motion of the boat beneath her feet grounded her in a way nothing else could. Mira wasn't beautiful in the conventional sense—her features were sharp, angular, but there was something striking about her, especially in the light. Her toned physique was the result of years of both rock climbing and sailing, a subtle strength that came from being connected to the earth and sea. The way the sun kissed her skin and how her sea-salt hair caught in the breeze made her look untouched by the world. She exuded quiet confidence and didn't need to be beautiful—which made her just that.

James, however, was still lost in his own world. He had tried to take the helm earlier, but he had neither the skill nor the patience for the boat, and nearly crash gybed them into a swim.

He'd laughed it off. "Temperamental little thing!"

She had humored him for a while, but it was clear from the start—he wasn't suited for the job. Mira had taken over again, her hands steady on the wheel.

"Maybe you should check the forecast," Mira suggested, her voice calm. The clouds were gathering off to the south, a faint darkness spreading across the horizon, and she could feel the air growing heavier.

James glanced at her briefly. "We've got time," he said, already dismissing the change.

Mira didn't argue. She trusted her instincts, something that had served her well over the years. Her grandfather's yacht, Siren, had taught her the art of listening to the sea and the sky.

The boat continued its course, but Mira noticed the wind picking up. It wasn't unusual in Autumn, but it felt more insistent, pushing harder against the sails. She adjusted the rigging, her hands moving automatically as she prepared for a shift in weather.

James had started to settle in, still too distracted by his phone to care about the growing tension in the air. She glanced back at him. "Maybe we should head back before it gets worse," she said, more to herself than to him. The forecast on her app had suggested clear weather, but she knew better than to trust it.

"Nothing to worry about, Mira," he replied with a casual wave of his hand.

Mira didn't answer immediately. She could see the storm now, dark clouds rolling in quickly from the west, the wind suddenly gusting harder. Her mind raced as she scanned the horizon, and that feeling—the one she always trusted—settled deep in her chest. Something was off.

She moved to adjust the sails, setting a more direct course to Paxos. The water, which had been peaceful, was now starting to show more agitation, the first signs of a shift in weather.

Mira's hands were steady on the wheel as she steered the boat, but inside, her thoughts were a whirlwind. This wasn't just a storm. The wind was coming in faster than it should have, and the pressure was dropping. Mira's instincts told her it wasn't just the weather she had to worry about. Something bigger was happening—something that wasn't just in the air.

James rose, took one last glance at the approaching clouds, and, on the pretext of getting more wine, disappeared below deck, leaving Mira alone at the helm.

As she adjusted the sails, her mind wandered, but only for a moment. She was too experienced to ignore the signs—too familiar with the way the sea could suddenly change its mood. She glanced at her phone once more, still reading clear weather, but the sinking feeling in her gut told her otherwise.

She adjusted the rudder again and tightened the sails, bracing for what was coming. The storm was no longer just a change in weather. It was a shift—in the sea, in the air, and perhaps, in the very world she thought she understood.

The first gust hit hard, and Mira immediately recognized it for what it was—a medicane, a rare storm system that could develop without warning in the Mediterranean. She'd seen it happen before.

The wind screamed across the deck, and the dark clouds that had been gathering quickly swallowed up the fading sunlight. Mira adjusted the wheel, steering Siren into the wind with the practiced ease of someone who had spent years on the water.

The sea churned, waves rising with a sudden intensity, as if the very ocean had been roused from a deep slumber. She moved quickly, pulling at the lines to reef the sails, reducing the boat's exposure to the increasing force of the wind. Siren leaned heavily, her hull cutting through the rising swell, the boat feeling like it was almost riding on the waves rather than slicing through them.

James, who had been below deck earlier, came stumbling up into the cockpit, his face pale, eyes wide with panic. "Mira!" he shouted over the howl of the wind, "What the hell's going on?!"

Mira barely glanced at him, her hands steady as she continued to adjust the sails. The medicane, came out of nowhere, quick and brutal, yet almost as quickly, it would pass. But during those few minutes, it could turn deadly.

The wind howled around them, heeling the boat to one side. Mira's hands gripped the wheel firmly, her feet bracing on the deck. She was used to this, having weathered storms in this region before, but it was always a reminder that the sea could turn on you in the blink of an eye.

James, on the other hand, was inexperienced at best, and seasick at worst. He stumbled around the cockpit, desperately clutching at the railing as the boat pitched and rolled, the waves crashing over the sides of the deck. His face went from green to ashen in seconds.

"Get down below!" Mira shouted over the noise, but it was too late. James was already retching over the side, barely managing to hold onto the boat as it tossed and turned with the wind.

The sails were now reefed tightly, but the storm wasn't finished with them yet. Mira quickly adjusted the boat's course, making sure they weren't heading into the wind directly, but even so, the waves were relentless. She had to keep them on a steady course and manage the rudder with precision, every second counting.

The wind screamed, whipping through the rigging as if it had a mind of its own, the storm bearing down on them like an unholy force. The rain came suddenly, sharp stinging sheets of it hitting her face and hands, making it nearly impossible to see. But Mira kept her focus, knowing exactly what to do: steady the course, watch the horizon, and ride out the storm.

James, still clutching the deck, now looked like he was on the verge of collapse, his knees giving way under the strain. Mira barely spared him a glance. He wasn't capable of dealing with this, and she'd known that from the moment he boarded.

As the wind intensified, the rain thickened, pouring in torrents, a wall of water blurring everything around them. But Mira, focused on the boat and her immediate surroundings, pushed through. The sails were nearly flattened, and Siren was responding well to the reduced pressure, cutting through the waves, but it felt like the boat was fighting against something more primal—nature itself.

Mira's jaw was set, her arms taut as she guided the wheel. There was a calmness about her, a quiet determination, even as the boat threatened to roll with the rising waves. She could feel it, the storm's intensity, but she was in control. She had to be.

The squall's full fury lasted only a few minutes, but in that time, it had done its damage. The rain and wind came to a screeching halt, leaving a dead silence in its wake, almost as if the storm had never happened.

Mira stood in the cockpit, breathing deeply as the wind began to die down. She adjusted the sails again, releasing the tension on the lines. The boat slowly leveled out as the water calmed, the last of the rain dripping from the rigging.

James, still bent over the edge of the cockpit, was now lying on the deck, looking like he had barely survived the ordeal. Mira didn't say anything. She had known what she was getting into. The sea had always been her domain, and it didn't wait for anyone to catch up.

"Are you okay?" she asked flatly, though she didn't expect a reply. She knew James was too dazed to respond. He barely mustered a nod, his face still pale, but his focus was already wandering back to his phone and how he would retell his experience on social media.

Mira shook her head slightly.

It had passed. For now, anyway.

But the storm wasn't the only thing Mira needed to worry about. There was a growing unease within her—a sense that something beyond the storm was coming, something far more dangerous than the wind or the waves.

Mira Grant had been working tirelessly as a reporter for the past two years, covering political stories and corporate corruption from the newsroom of a prestigious San Francisco-based publication. As a journalist with a background in computer programming, she had been drawn to investigative work that mixed both technology and human stories. Her writing was sharp, analytical, and often at the forefront of stories that challenged public opinion and institutional narratives.

It was a grueling career, but one Mira had always known she would pursue. From the moment she finished her studies at university, she'd felt a call to expose the truth, no matter how inconvenient or uncomfortable it might be. She had studied communications with a minor in computer science, a combination that had made her uniquely qualified to understand both the technical and human sides of the stories she wrote.

At university, she had learned the art of critical thinking, digging into systems to see how they worked and, more importantly, how they failed. Her fascination with the intersection of technology and society had been sparked in her first semester when she took a class on digital ethics. By the time she graduated, she knew she would be working in journalism—but with a focus on the technological influences that were beginning to shape global politics, media, and daily life.

Her reporting had quickly gained traction, and within a year, she was covering high-stakes stories on tech companies, government surveillance, and media manipulation. She had made a name for herself by digging into the underground operations of the tech world, examining how corporate giants shaped both the economy and society through data collection and influence.

But it hadn't been easy. The grind of working as a reporter had worn her down. Deadlines and burnout had begun to take their toll, and after months of reporting on conflict, she had decided she needed a break—a brief escape to clear her head and reconnect with herself. The Mediterranean Sea had always been a place of solace for her, so when the opportunity for a one-week break arrived, Mira jumped at the chance.

It had been a last-minute decision, but the moment she arrived in Corfu, Mira felt the weight lifted off her shoulders. Here, on Siren, she was reminded of the simplicity and independence she had imagined long ago as a way of life. The quiet, steady hum of the boat's movement in the water soothed her. The absence of manmade noise on Siren was a stark contrast to the hum of constant information, the endless notifications, and the relentless demands of her reporting job back in San Francisco.

Mira guided Siren into the sheltered bay of Gaios, the main harbor of Paxos. The storm had passed as quickly as it had arrived, leaving a heavy, wet calm in its wake. The water had settled into a soft, rhythmic lapping against the hull, and the sky was beginning to clear, revealing the dimming outline of the Ionian Islands.

Her hands were steady on the wheel, and her movements were calm—almost meditative, as she brought the boat in. The familiar motion of navigating Siren into its dock felt like home. Despite the unexpected squall, she was accustomed to the unpredictable nature of the sea. She trusted herself.

James, on the other hand, hadn't fared as well. After the storm passed, he had spent the rest of the time below deck, nursing his seasickness and trying to steady himself after the violent waves. The contrast between them couldn't have been clearer.

As Mira secured the lines and eased the boat into position, James finally emerged from below deck, looking as though the ordeal had taken everything out of him. His face was still pale, and his hair was tousled, his usual charm completely absent.

"Thanks for the trip," he said weakly, forcing a grin. "I guess I'm not cut out for sailing after all."

Mira didn't smile back. She was tired—not just physically, but emotionally. She had known this trip, this encounter, was always meant to be temporary, an escape from her grind in San Francisco. James had served his purpose in distracting her for a short time, but as always, she couldn't help but feel that he was just another person who came into her life, using her as a stepping stone before finding their next destination.

"I'm glad you're feeling better," Mira said, her voice a touch colder than she intended.

James seemed to sense the finality in her words. He looked at her for a moment, as if trying to gauge whether she was just being polite or whether this was, in fact, the end. His eyes flicked briefly to the boat before he sighed, a mixture of frustration and resignation in his gaze.

"I'll take a walk into the village." he said. There was no attempt to offer any form of goodbye beyond the few words.

Mira nodded, not trusting herself to say anything else. The finality of it all felt almost relieving—he would leave, and she could have the space she needed. As he walked away down the dock, Mira felt a deep sense of solitude, but it wasn't the loneliness she feared. It was the kind of solitude that meant she could finally breathe.

As the sound of his footsteps faded, Mira turned back toward the boat. The harbor was quiet now, save for the gentle sound of the water. She untied the ropes and adjusted the lines, ensuring everything was secure for the night. There was a strange peace in the air, despite the storm earlier. The familiar gurgling of the Mediterranean filled the space around her, the evening breeze now soft and cool against her skin.

With James gone, Mira settled into the small but comfortable cabin of Siren. She switched on a dim light and sat down at the small table, allowing herself a moment to reflect. The quiet of the boat, surrounded by nothing but the sea and the distant land, felt like a balm for her soul. Inside the cabin, the smell of coffee and salt lingered. She lit the small stove, boiling water as she peeled off her soaked clothes and hung them above the berth to dry. Her muscles ached pleasantly and she rubbed her bare shoulder while pouring the steaming water into her primed French coffee press.

She pulled her phone from her bag, checking the messages she had ignored all day. Her inbox was full—news updates, work-related emails, and the usual flow of information she had left behind. She scrolled through them absently, not in the mood to engage. Her focus, instead, was still on the sea—the calm after the storm. She felt untethered, free from the endless cycle of deadlines and corporate agendas.

The small kitchen warmed up quickly and she found a moment of peace as she sipped from the mug, gazing out the window. The view of the harbor, lit by the faint glow of distant lanterns, looked almost like a painting. The world seemed to slow here, away from the chaos of the city and the ever-present noise of modern life.

For a moment, it felt like everything was in its right place.

She took another sip of coffee.

Her grandfather's old journal sat in a drawer beside the berth. She pulled it out, flipping through the water-stained pages. He'd kept meticulous notes—weather patterns, sailing routes, overheard conversations from taverns that read like spy novels.

She found one entry from March, 1986:

"Spoke to a man in Piraeus who said the future of war isn't bombs—it's newspapers. Whoever controls the truth wins. Strange thing to hear over ouzo."

Mira traced the ink with her finger. Some truths aged better than others.

She closed the journal and stretched out on the bench, feeling the gentle sway of the boat beneath her. The sky outside was clearing, stars beginning to blink into view.

But as the night stretched on, Mira couldn't shake the feeling that something was stirring—not just the sea, but the world around her. Her work in journalism had always driven her to uncover the truths hidden beneath the surface, but now, as she sat on this boat in the dark, a new feeling was rising in her chest: a sensation that whatever she was about to face, it was going to be much larger than she had anticipated.

She set her phone down, resolved to deal with the world tomorrow. For now, Mira closed her eyes and allowed herself to rest—for just one night—on the boat her grandfather had once sailed, the only true place where she could escape.

But she could still hear it—the faintest hum of the siren's call in the distance, beckoning her forward.

Two

Echo Chamber

The morning came softly, the first light of dawn casting a pale golden hue over the Ionian Sea. The quiet of the harbor was undisturbed, the faint ripple of water against the hull of Siren the only sound. Mira had slept well—deeper than she had in weeks—but now, the pull of the new day beckoned her.

The boat was still and secure, the sun warming the deck as she stretched and stood, feeling the calmness of the morning settle into her bones. The storm was now a memory, and the world seemed to return to its natural rhythm. She grabbed a light jacket and stepped out onto the deck, the air fresh with the promise of a new day.

Mira decided to take a walk. She needed to stretch her legs and clear her mind before the day began. The streets of Paxos were still quiet, with only a few early risers walking along the cobblestone lanes. Mira enjoyed the solitude of the island's gentle rhythm—everything felt still, at peace, like time slowed here.

She walked along the small path leading out of the harbor, the low hum of distant voices in the town blending with the occasional creak of fishing boats rocking gently in the bay. After a while, she reached the small dockside café, where she grabbed a coffee, the steam rising from the cup into the cool morning air.

Her phone buzzed in her pocket, and she pulled it out, squinting at the screen.

Victoria had texted: "I'm at Corfu airport. Flight just landed—catch you in 30min? Will be at the terminal."

Mira smiled to herself. Victoria. The one person who had always been able to keep up with her—the one person who hadn't faded from her life, despite the years. They had met in their first semester at university, thrown together in a required computer science course. Mira had been the sharper coder, but Victoria had a strategic mind for systems that always impressed her. While Mira veered into journalism with a tech lens, Victoria went deeper into IT and cybersecurity. They bonded quickly, not just over shared interests but over hours spent at the university's rock climbing wall and outside, chalk dust and adrenaline between them. There had been one climb in particular— outdoors, on a new route - Victoria had dropped her belay device high on a ledge, panic rising fast—but Mira's calm, measured voice had talked her through a makeshift anchor and a safe descent. It was the kind of experience that cemented trust for life.

When Mira had decided to take a week off in Greece, Victoria had jumped at the chance to catch up, even if only for a day or two.

It had been a long time since they'd shared space in this way.

Mira felt a twinge of excitement, something familiar and warm, as she made her way back to Siren and packed up a small bag for her trip to the airport. The walk felt shorter now, her thoughts already moving toward Victoria. There was a spark between them, something unspoken, but never fully acknowledged. It had always been there, lingering just under the surface. It was impossible to ignore.

Corfu Airport, Ioannis Kapodistrias

The airport was small, the occasional flight announcement echoing through the terminal as Mira made her way through the crowd. She noticed the usual chaos at the check-in counters, the flurry of travelers all moving in their own directions. She couldn't help but overhear the conversation between a couple of passengers discussing how their flight had been delayed again.

"Typical," one of them muttered. "This airline's always late. It's like clockwork. I swear their share price will never recover if this continues."

Mira raised an eyebrow at the casual remark. She had always been fascinated by the interplay of business and daily life—how something so insignificant, like a late flight, could ripple through a company's financial health. But it was just an aside—nothing more than background noise to her mind, which was now firmly focused on the small crowd waiting in the terminal.

And then she saw her.

Victoria stood near the baggage claim, her dark hair tied back in a messy bun, wearing a simple green jacket and jeans. Her stance was familiar and relaxed, but the moment their eyes met, a shift occurred. A subtle change in the air, as if time itself had slowed, just for them.

Mira's breath caught for a split second. It was always like that when they saw each other after time apart—a quiet pull, a gravity that couldn't quite be explained.

Victoria's lips curled into a smile, and her eyes sparkled with the same mischief that Mira remembered so well. "It's been too long," she said softly, her voice low, with a hint of that unmistakable accent that Mira loved.

Mira walked over, feeling the familiarity settle between them. She stood a little too close, not sure why it felt so natural. As if the space between them had never quite existed. Her gaze lingered on Victoria's face—her striking features, the sharpness of her jawline, the intensity in her eyes.

"You look… amazing," Mira said, voice soft, not quite able to hide the warmth in her words.

Victoria smirked, her eyes glinting with something just between them. She stepped closer and wrapped Mira in a quick but familiar hug.

"You too, as always," Victoria replied, her hug lingering just a beat longer than necessary.

They fell into step together, walking toward the exit of the terminal, both of them comfortable in the quiet rhythm of the moment.

"You should become a travel agent," Mira teased, referencing Victoria's uncanny ability to find the last seat on a flight at the drop of a hat.

Victoria shrugged, the glint in her eyes still playful. "I like finding the unfindable. Like you do with your investigations." Her voice dropped slightly as she glanced at Mira sideways. "And I couldn't help but notice your reports about the tech firms. You've been busy."

Mira raised an eyebrow but didn't comment, knowing full well what Victoria was referring to. She had been diving into corporate tech manipulations, just beginning to connect the dots. But this wasn't the time for that.

"Maybe I've been a little too busy," Mira said, her voice quieter now. "It's good to step away for a bit."

Victoria's smile softened, and the chemistry between them deepened for a moment—something warm, something unspoken, but understood.

"I'm glad you did," Victoria said, as they stepped outside the airport doors into the bright, sunlit Corfu day.

The walk to the restaurant took them through the winding streets of Corfu Town, the narrow alleys lined with cafes and small boutiques. Ivy clung to the weathered walls, and old shutters creaked in the warm breeze. The pace was slow—unhurried—as they strolled through the sun-dappled streets, the cobblestones warm beneath their feet.

When they reached the small tavern tucked away in a quiet corner, the clatter of pans and the distant hum of a radio playing traditional folk music filled the air. The restaurant had the charm of an old family-run establishment, its wooden tables shaded by a large, wisteria-covered trellis. It was a spot where the locals gathered, a place that offered comfort and tradition with every meal.

They were seated at a table by the open window, where the light filtered through the vines in soft dappled patterns. The gentle murmur of voices from neighbouring tables blended with the clinking of glasses and the scrape of cutlery on ceramic plates.

The waiter, a middle-aged man with a thick moustache, came by with a basket of warm pita bread and a small bowl of tzatziki. Mira picked up a piece of bread, dipping it into the sauce.

Her features were Greek enough to pass for a local—high cheekbones, olive-toned skin, eyes that caught the light like sea glass. As she spoke to the waiter, her accent stumbled only slightly. Her Greek was rusty, but serviceable, and she spoke with a quiet confidence that drew a smile from the man as he walked away.

A few minutes later, they ordered their main courses. Victoria went for a local white wine, a crisp, dry Assyrtiko, while Mira opted for sparkling water, not touching alcohol. She had usually been the sober one—focused, grounded—particularly when she had something important on her mind. Today was no different.

"Same as always, huh?" Victoria teased as the waiter poured wine into her glass, the liquid gleaming in the light.

Mira smiled softly. "I prefer to keep a clear head."

"I know," Victoria said, with a hint of something teasing in her tone, before taking a long sip from her glass. "Guess someone's gotta stay sober enough to pull me out of trouble."

They both laughed. The easy rhythm between them was still there, intact despite the months apart.

Mira leaned back in her chair and glanced around the restaurant. It was starting to fill now—older men exchanging morning gossip over espresso, a pair of German tourists thumbing through a worn guidebook, a small boy darting between tables as his mother called after him. The scene was ordinary, yet grounding. It made her feel briefly like she was watching a simpler world, one not yet distorted by headlines and algorithms.

"I think I could live here," Mira said.

Victoria looked at her with quiet amusement. "You say that every time you leave the city."

"I know," Mira replied. "But this time, it feels different."

Victoria tilted her head. "Because you're actually considering it? Or because you're finally tired?"

Mira didn't answer at first. She broke off another piece of bread, more to delay than to eat. Then she said, "Maybe both."

Victoria leaned forward slightly, her voice quieter now. "You always burned hotter than the rest of us. Didn't matter if it was coursework or climbing or chasing a lead—you never half-assed anything."

Mira gave a tired smile. "And look where that got me."

"It got you here," Victoria said, gesturing around them, "on a Greek island, with time to breathe. Most people never even get that far."

There was a long pause as Mira looked out the window. Beyond the vines and sunlit courtyard, a stray cat lazed on a stone step, blinking slowly at the world.

"Sometimes I wonder if I mistook motion for meaning," she said finally. "Always chasing, always reporting. Like if I stopped, everything would collapse."

Victoria didn't respond immediately. When she did, her voice was steady. "You're not collapsing now. You're resting."

They sat quietly after that, the clatter of cutlery and the low murmur of Greek voices filling the space between them. It was a small moment, unremarkable by any outside measure, yet Mira felt something shift—a loosening in her chest, a softness she rarely let herself feel.

"Tell me," she said, reaching for her glass of water, "what's the least boring thing that's happened to you in the past six months?"

Victoria grinned. "Define boring."

And just like that, the mood lightened again. But Mira knew it wouldn't last. Something was coming—something she couldn't quite name yet. And when it did, she'd need every ounce of that old focus again.

For now, though, she listened.

Just a few streets away, inside a shaded café, Giannis , a local bank employee, sat with his laptop open. The screen glowed with market data and finance articles—his daily ritual. He clicked on an opinion piece: "The Stock Market's Unseen Risks: Why Experts Are Forecasting a Major Correction." Another article followed—bleaker, more specific. The forecasts felt closer than before, more targeted. Giannis furrowed his brow, hovered over his investment dashboard, and shifted a chunk of his modest savings into defensive stocks. It was precaution, he told himself.

Across town, Katerina, a retired nurse, scrolled through her phone from the balcony of her quiet apartment. Between photos of her grandkids and a forwarded video of a local choir, one link stood out. It led to an article about protests in Athens—fiery rhetoric about national sovereignty, veiled accusations about foreign influence. She clicked, then clicked again—another article, then a fundraiser. It wasn't much, but she donated. A small gesture, she told herself. A way to support the country's future. She didn't feel radical. Just awake.

And in a tucked-away bar near the harbour, the shadows played differently. David , a Greek-American expat, sat nursing a beer beside Elena his Ukrainian-born girlfriend. The neon light above them flickered, and the voices from the nearby table grew louder—men in their fifties, speaking in low, pointed tones about foreigners, about "taking back" Corfu. David didn't respond, but he listened. Something in him stirred, something old and restless, a memory of identity that felt half-claimed. Elena touched his arm gently. "Let's go," she said. Outside, under the clear Corfu sky, David paused. "I didn't expect to hear that here," he murmured. "It makes me think..." Elena nodded, not looking back. "That's what worries me."

As the afternoon waned and the light softened, Mira and Victoria wandered back through the narrow streets, stopping to pick up bread, olives, and a few ripe tomatoes from the local market. Back at the harbour, Siren waited quietly, rocking gently against her lines. They settled in on board as the sky deepened to gold, unpacking their groceries, sharing stories in low voices as the shadows lengthened. Mira rarely let people into that space overnight—Siren had always been her own quiet sanctuary—but having Victoria there felt natural. There was something grounding in knowing the boat was still hers, yet now carrying more than just solitude. But even that peace came with a whisper. Siren had always felt like refuge, but tonight she felt like invitation. Not escape, exactly. A summons. The kind that didn't come from the sea, but from something deeper—something that moved just beneath the surface, calling Mira forward again.

Three

Residuals

Their time together had felt like a lifetime. The sea air, the quiet swaying of Siren beneath her feet, and the late-night conversations with Victoria had given Mira a rare sense of peace. It had been a long time since she'd allowed herself the luxury of real downtime—free from deadlines, from news cycles, from the relentless edge of her career. The hum of constant alerts, of curated chaos in her inbox, had faded. Here, surrounded by sea and cypress, she could breathe. She could remember who she was without the constant pressure to produce, to expose, to run.

Those two days had unfolded slowly, like warm honey. They had wandered the narrow backstreets of Gaios together, slipping between whitewashed buildings and shuttered stone homes with bright blue trim. Mira led Victoria to a tiny café she'd frequented with her grandfather years ago, where the owner—a wiry man named Stavros—greeted them like family, with briki-brewed coffee and almonds. They sat in the shade of a fig tree, watching fishermen mend their nets along the harbor's edge, their fingers deft and unhurried.

Later, they browsed the town's open-air market. Mira admired a weathered volume of poetry in Greek she couldn't quite translate anymore, and Victoria bartered for a string of dried oregano and a packet of saffron. They bought fresh fruit from a wooden stall manned by a silent old woman, and local silver earrings that Victoria convinced Mira to try on—"just to see"—before insisting they were too perfect not to buy. Mira had laughed, a full, real laugh that felt like it came from a deeper place than usual.

They sat at a beachside tavern with their feet in the sand and a dish of grilled octopus between them. The wine made them drowsy, and for a while, they just listened to the waves roll in. That afternoon, they sailed to a cove Mira had wanted to visit before the storm. Victoria pulled off her clothes and dove in without hesitation, her limbs cutting effortlessly through the still, cerulean water. Mira followed more slowly, her body relishing the feeling of salt water, warmth, and flickering light. Floating on her back, she watched Victoria tread water in silence, framed by the jagged rocks and sky.

There was something easy about their time together, the kind of rhythm that came from deep familiarity and rare time alone. They fell into an old pattern quickly—a shorthand built on years of friendship, threaded with something that neither had ever named aloud.

That night, they cooked a simple meal aboard Siren—grilled vegetables, crusty bread, fresh olive oil, and big chunks of local cheese. They talked well into the early hours, sprawled on deck cushions, sharing stories half-remembered from university and long-forgotten assignments that had somehow led them here: two women at the edge of the world, caught somewhere between then and now. When Mira mentioned a professor neither of them liked, Victoria laughed so hard she snorted, and Mira found herself laughing just as hard—not because the story was that funny, but because it felt so good to remember.

The world beyond the sea felt far away. For a moment, Mira had even begun to believe she could stay.

But as always, peace was fleeting.

Late in the afternoon of their second day, Victoria was below deck, unpacking a few more finds from the local shops—olive soap, beeswax lip balm, a jar of capers—when Mira's phone buzzed.

It was Lena.

She answered. "Hey."

"Mira," Lena said immediately, her voice taut. "We've got a situation. You need to hear this."

Within moments, the old world snapped back into focus. The Indian startup—Vedanta AI—had collapsed. Investors had fled in droves, their confidence gutted by a sudden barrage of accusations. Anonymous leaks. Whispers of espionage. Military-grade predictive algorithms. The government had yet to issue a formal statement, but the damage was done.

"But wait for it: Epsilon Tech - They swooped in and bought it all," Lena said. "Everything. The data, the codebase, even the R&D teams. Like they were waiting for it."

Mira's jaw tightened. "Are you saying the collapse was engineered?"

"I'm saying it's too perfect. This wasn't a crash. This was a controlled demolition."

Mira walked to the bow as Lena kept talking. The Ionian wind lifted her hair, the sea glittered peacefully—utterly indifferent. The juxtaposition struck her—how calm the sea was, how violent the information she was hearing felt. Her reporter's instinct snapped back to life, like a dormant circuit reconnected.

"And here's the kicker," Lena said. "Epsilon's CEO is giving a keynote in two days. Barcelona. The Global AI Summit."

Mira was already checking her calendar. "I want press accreditation. Can you push it through?"

"I'll pull every string I have," Lena said. "But you'll need to move."

"I know."

After the call, Mira opened her travel app and booked a one-way flight out of Corfu the next morning. She reserved a small hotel room in Barcelona—quiet, functional, familiar to foreign press. Then she fired off an email to Niko, the harbourhand.

Subject: Quick Change of Plans

Hey Niko, something urgent's come up. I'll be flying out early tomorrow, and I've secured the lines as usual. Would you mind checking on Siren once or twice while I'm gone? I'll transfer a little something for your trouble. Efharistó, file mou.

– Mira

She set the phone down slowly, fingers lingering on the deck rail. The light was starting to turn orange-gold, and the hum of cicadas began to rise from the hills beyond the harbor.

Mira stayed at the rail for a long moment after sending the email. The sea had begun to darken slightly, shifting to indigo under the fading light. In the distance, a fishing boat chugged slowly across the mouth of the bay, its engine a dull murmur. The contrast between the simplicity of the scene and the complexity unraveling in her mind felt almost unbearable.

She exhaled sharply and rolled her shoulders. Her world had pivoted again, and she could already feel the thread of the story tugging at her, insistent and inescapable.

Victoria emerged from below deck holding two small cups of Greek coffee.

"You look like you've just declared war," she said lightly, handing one to Mira.

Mira hesitated. "I'm flying to Barcelona in the morning. There's a tech conference. Epsilon will be there and I need to figure out what they are doing."

Victoria didn't look surprised. She simply nodded, then leaned against the rail beside her. A moment passed.

"So it's starting," she said.

Mira didn't answer. Her mind was already racing—threading names, timelines, keywords, suspicions. But something in her chest ached.

The sun began its descent, casting long ribbons of gold over the harbor. The boats in the marina creaked gently against their moorings. The smell of charcoal from a nearby grill drifted over the water.

They stood in silence, sipping coffee, dusk settling on their skin. Mira let her shoulder lean into Victoria's just slightly.

Victoria reached out, gently taking Mira's hand.

"We have one more night," she said, her voice soft but steady. "Let's make the most of it."

Mira turned toward her, and for the first time since the call, she let herself smile.

Calibration

The plane banked low over the Mediterranean, its wing slicing cleanly through a gauze of late afternoon cloud. From her window seat, Mira watched as Barcelona unfurled beneath her in geometric intricacy. From this height, the city resembled a circuit board—tight grids of terracotta rooftops and pale concrete shot through with arteries of green. In the distance, the hills of Montjuïc rolled gently upward, and the glittering sea edged the city like a blade.

Closer now, she spotted the Sagrada Família's jagged spires breaching the skyline, cranes still hanging above like scaffolding left behind by giants. The plane's gentle tilt gave her a clear view of the marina below, the docks a latticework of white, blue, and chrome. Somewhere down there, people were living their quiet daily dramas. Dogs barking, shutters clattering open, wine glasses catching the last of the sun. It all felt oddly distant, like watching a diorama through glass.

But Mira was used to that feeling. Observation had always been her role.

Her thoughts drifted, unbidden, back to the airport on Corfu.

Victoria had hugged her a little too tightly, the pressure soft but lingering. Mira had memorised the scent of her—suncream, fig leaves, and salt. They hadn't spoken about when they would see each other again.

The words had hovered between them, unspoken. Mira had promised to text once she landed. Victoria had nodded, smile subdued, gaze evasive. It had been a goodbye without punctuation.

The wheels touched down with a muted jolt. Barcelona.

She moved through El Prat swiftly, travelling light. Her grey canvas backpack contained the essentials: a few changes of clothes, her laptop, a field recorder, noise-cancelling headphones, her encrypted hard drive, chargers, two notebooks, a jumble of pens, and her water bottle—a battered silver one she'd had since university, covered in faded stickers and dents from years of use.

She cleared customs, bypassed the luggage carousels, and stepped into the dry Catalonian heat. It was too early to check into her hotel, but not too early to make her presence known.

The conference centre sat in a glimmering quarter of the city—half steel-and-glass futurism, half landscaped fantasy. It looked like a spaceship that had settled gently into the earth and decided to stay. The Global AI Futures Congress was already in full swing, its signage blazoned across every available surface: Humanity Forward: Converging on Intelligence.

Mira hated it on sight.

Inside, the air was aspirational Scandinavian—crisp, overchilled, while the walls were lined with projection screens showcasing pulsating neural nets, bouncing stock graphs, and abstract data blooms. A young woman with a badge scanner waved Mira toward a media registration desk.

"Name?"

"Mira Grant. Fourth Estate. I pre-registered."

The woman tapped quickly, smiled, and passed her a laminated press badge.

"Here you go. Let us know if you want your tracking enabled. It helps us streamline delegate experience."

"I'll pass," Mira replied, already clipping it to her jacket.

The badge had an embedded RFID chip, standard issue. It would allow the organisers to track foot traffic, dwell time, engagement zones—whatever jargon they preferred. She knew the kind. She also knew better than to willingly be followed. One small refusal. One tick box unchecked.

She stepped into the main hall and made her way to a water station. Her throat was dry from the flight, and her eyes ached from the glare of backlit signage. She filled her bottle from the cooler, the water glugging loudly into the steel. As she turned, sipping slowly, she scanned the room.

Clusters of tech royalty had already gathered. She spotted Mitchell Caine from Halcyon Robotics, grinning as he greeted a rotating gallery of handlers. His tailored jacket shimmered faintly in the light, some smart-fabric nonsense that adjusted to room temperature. Two assistants hovered near him, one holding a portable monitor, the other feeding him names and facial recognition data through a discreet earpiece.

Not far off, an upstart CEO from Seoul was giving an impromptu demo to a crowd of fawning bloggers. Her model claimed to simulate human grief responses in digital avatars. The crowd applauded, but Mira caught the dead look behind the CEO's smile. Performance, all of it.

A tall man in a salmon blazer shouted over a live-stream panel about "post-symbolic cognition," while nearby, a woman in sequins and combat boots was busy explaining why her venture—a decentralised, blockchain-based AI monastery—was the "spiritual upgrade Silicon Valley needed."

Mira rolled her eyes.

And then she saw him.

Elias Stein.

He stood alone near the base of a sculpture that looked like a cross between a torus and a Möbius strip. No entourage. No cameras. Just a slim, grey blazer, soft-soled shoes, and a tired expression that did little to disguise the intensity behind his eyes. He moved with quiet purpose, pausing to check a screen at one of the side exhibits.

He looked older than his 38 years. Not in the Hollywood sense of age, but in the way people who carried too much knowledge did. His hair was streaked with silver, his posture a little stooped, like he'd learned to listen harder than he spoke. Mira had seen enough CEOs to know when someone was pretending to be humble.

Elias wasn't pretending.

Something about him felt displaced. As though he'd wandered in from a better, more deliberate time. There were no handlers shadowing him. No product launch banners. Just the quiet man at the eye of a storm.

Mira didn't approach. Not yet. She watched him melt back into the corridor, swallowed by mirrored walls and motion-sensing lights.

She pulled out the conference schedule. Her eyes flicked down to the keynote list.

Epsilon Systems: "Distributed Cognition in the Public Sphere"
10:00 AM. Main Hall. Saturday.

Tomorrow.

Nothing else today looked especially vital. Some panel on bio-ethics in swarm learning. A workshop on storytelling with GPT avatars. The usual theatre.

She headed for the exit.

The sunlight was harsher now, bouncing off the glass plaza. She was halfway across it, fumbling in her pocket for her phone, when a voice called out.

"Mira! Mira Grant?"

She turned.

A man about her age trotted toward her, bag slung haphazardly over one shoulder, curly hair flattened by travel sweat. He looked like he'd been running on fumes and hope for three years straight.

"Eli Navarro," he said, panting slightly. "We met in Berlin? That panel on algorithmic bias in electoral systems?"

"Of course," Mira said. "Still running your startup?"

He laughed. "Still trying. We're finally onto something, though. A speech model that nails local dialects and regional accents. Like, scary accurate. Emotional tone, breathing patterns, colloquialisms—we call it Vocalite."

"Sounds potent."

"It is! You should hear yourself read back with a Dublin cadence. It's uncanny. We're in G9 tomorrow. You should swing by."

He paused, "Drinks tonight if you're free?"

She smiled, more politely than warmly. "Appreciate the invite, but I'm under water with research."

He took it well. "Totally. Still good to see you."

She nodded and moved on.

The hotel room was compact, clean, and unmemorable—exactly what she preferred. Mira tossed her bag onto the bed, peeled off her clothes, and stepped into the shower. The water came hot and fast, steaming the small cubicle, the city sliding off her skin. She scrubbed the travel from her shoulders and tilted her face into the stream, eyes closed.

Wrapped in a towel, she padded barefoot to the bed, hair damp and curling at the ends. She lay on her back, phone on her chest, screen glowing dimly.

She opened a new message to Victoria.

Landed. Barcelona's loud, overdesigned, and full of people who think AI will save us from ourselves.

A minute passed.

Victoria replied.

Sounds perfect for you. Soothing, really.

Mira smiled faintly.

I miss the boat already.

I miss the quiet.

Another pause.

I miss you, Mira typed. Then, impulsively, Even if you hogged the deck cushions.

Deck hogging is a form of love, came the reply.

Let me know when you're back, Victoria added. Not "if."

Mira's fingers hovered over the screen. Her chest ached a little.

I will.

The reply came almost instantly.

Good.

She stared at the phone, then placed it face down beside her and closed her eyes as her towel slipped off her shoulder.

Her moment of reflection was interrupted. A call was coming in.

Mark Benning. San Francisco. It was 9:34 a.m. there. He had probably been in the office since 7am.

She answered.

His voice was gravel and morning warmth. "Mira. You made it."

She sat up, tightening her towel instinctively.

"Barcelona. It's a zoo."

"I figured," he said. "I've seen the roster. Looks like the future's having a cosplay convention."

Mark had been in the game far longer than most. Late fifties now, steel-grey hair and a face lined not with stress but with observation. He'd started in tech reporting when tech reporting meant modem manuals and start-ups in garages. Mira had read his columns in university, then interned under him at Signal. He had taught her the difference between a trend and a movement. He'd also taught her when to keep her mouth shut—and when to dig so hard they couldn't ignore her.

He was the closest thing she had to a mentor. Possibly the only editor she still trusted.

"You're watching Epsilon, right?" he said.

"Already spotted Stein. No handlers. No noise. He's... unnerving."

Mark grunted. "Yeah. They say he meditates before code reviews. And walks barefoot through server rooms to check grounding."

"Seriously?"

"No. But wouldn't that be something?"

They both laughed.

A beat passed. Mark's tone softened.

"Be careful, Mira. This story feels like it wants to be written. But some stories write back."

She closed her eyes for a moment.

"I know."

"I'll be here," he added. "If you need another pair of eyes. Or someone to talk you down."

"I'll probably need both."

"Good," he said. "Means you're still human. Keep me in the loop."

The call ended. Mira sat in silence for a moment, then reached for her laptop.

The Wi-Fi was sluggish but passable. She logged onto her VPN and then opened the Duckduckgo search engine and typed: Epsilon India. Vedanta AI. Collapse.

Pages of results poured in. Most were regurgitations of the official line. A failed Indian startup. Shareholder exodus. Epsilon's swift acquisition of key assets. The same story rewritten a thousand ways.

But there were cracks in the narrative.

An archived tweet hinted that Vedanta's models had begun self-editing.

A buried blog from an ex-contractor suggested Vedanta had been experimenting with "speculative memory structures" in its neural frameworks. Constructs that simulated regret. Another claimed the language models had begun to "protect" certain training data.

And then the name: Sandhya Patel. Vedanta's former CTO. Vanished post-collapse. No updates. No public statement. LinkedIn dormant.

Mira made a list in her encrypted notes:

Track down Sandhya Patel

Timeline of Vedanta collapse

Financial pathways to Epsilon

Were Indian regulators coerced?

Why did Epsilon move so fast?

Any internal leaks? Whistleblowers?

She rubbed her eyes and leaned back in the chair, then sent a voice note to Lena asking her to see what she could dig up stateside.

Outside, Barcelona's sounds filtered in—muffled music, a scooter whining in the street, the faint rattle of plates from a distant bar. Inside, only the glow of her laptop and the distant, electric hum of something much larger moving beneath the surface.

In a noisy bar near Plaça del Sol, a young man named Mateo was livestreaming again—third night in a row. The glow of hearts and emojis scrolled across his phone as he broke down "secret market cycles" his followers claimed had predicted two recent crypto jumps. What he didn't mention was the AI tool he'd used to generate the pattern. It had no name—just a URL and a login—passed through a closed Telegram group. His voice grew more confident the longer the stream ran. Behind his smile, his eyes flicked constantly to the metrics: viewer retention, spike rate, monetisable chatter. Truth had become irrelevant. Only performance remained.

Across town, in a shared dormitory in El Raval, fourteen-year-old Hana sat on her lower bunk, watching short-form clips on loop. Climate panic. Beauty tips. A protest in Madrid. A conspiracy about food additives. A whispered confession from someone claiming to be a whistle-blower. Her thumb moved automatically, scroll after scroll, her gaze unfocused. Somewhere between the clips, she had clicked "yes" to a survey about trust and fear. She didn't remember doing it, but now, the feed felt... different. Quieter. Sharper. More seductive. Her brother called from the next room, but she didn't hear him.

On a rooftop terrace overlooking Carrer de Casp, a woman named Leila sat alone with her tablet, a half-finished beer warming beside her. She worked for an NGO. Had for years. But lately her inbox had filled with fringe reports, coordinated outrage, and alarming stats that didn't appear on official dashboards. She wasn't sure when she'd subscribed to the feed. The articles came daily, tailored and urgent. Some of them contradicted her training. But they felt truer. More visceral. The comments below them echoed what she'd started to feel—that something was broken. That someone had known all along.

Tomorrow, Elias Stein would speak.

And Mira Grant would be listening.

Five

Chorus

Mira's sleep had been broken—fitful snapshots of dreams that dissolved upon waking. Her body ached not from exertion, but from tension. Morning came anyway, light slicing into the corners of the hotel room like the edge of a blade. She blinked and reached for her phone.

Emails. Texts. One voice message from Lena.

_"Sandhya Patel is in Switzerland. Town's called Ftan—tiny village tucked away in the Lower Engadine Valley. Took a favour chain to trace her: friend of a friend working at a private charter jet company. Turns out Patel took a flight—then a helicopter—to Ftan the day after the board meeting. She's supposedly doing a silent meditation retreat. Off-grid. No contact. Guess who paid for the flights? The same company that manages Epsilon's corporate travel. Maybe it was part of the settlement, maybe they wanted her out of the limelight for a while. It's off the record, I promised I wouldn't mention them in this, but it's legit.

Also, here's what I've pieced together on Vedanta. They were fragile. Standard startup stuff: burn rate rising, Series B delays, cash flow issues. But the timing? Investors pulled out fast—too fast. Rumours spread like someone wanted a run. Confidence shattered overnight. They couldn't make payroll. A week later, nothing left. Either someone planted poison—or the wolves just smelled blood.

Also, there's one more lead... will send deets when I've triple-checked."_

Ftan. Mira pulled up an image: mountains pinned with snow, firs clustering around wooden chalets, paths stitched through silence. The kind of place you go to vanish.

Mira let the phone slip from her fingers and rose, stretching her arms. A low ache settled in her chest—a weight she hadn't noticed until she moved. It wasn't the news. It was the steady accumulation of things she couldn't quite name: missed chances, vague guilt, the feeling that something vital was shifting beneath her feet and she hadn't moved fast enough.

In the shower, steam filled the tiny cubicle, clinging to the mirror, fogging her outline. The water pounded hot against her shoulders, a cascade she welcomed. Soap slid down her skin, and she watched as it circled the drain—spiralling, tightening, vanishing. That whirlpool, fleeting and precise, gave her a strange sense of calm. A small, perfect system. Unlike everything else.

She towelled off and pulled on a charcoal-grey dress, the colour she always wore when she needed to be in a front-facing reporter mode. But this time she didn't aim to stand out. Quite the opposite.

Barcelona pulsed as Mira walked through its morning hum—graffiti-tagged shutters rising, scooters whining into motion, the scent of strong coffee and tobacco weaving through narrow lanes. The city's layered heartbeat echoed beneath her boots, uneven and alive.

The Global AI Futures Congress sprawled across the convention complex like a monument to ambition. Inside, reality blurred. A humanoid robot in a tuxedo sat before a grand piano, performing a Chopin nocturne with unsettling precision. Each note was mathematically perfect, the tempo shifts algorithmically derived from models trained on recordings of mourning. A small boy stood a few feet from the piano, utterly still, entranced. His mother filmed him watching—not the music, not the robot, but him.

Mira paused, watching too. The child's fascination was pure. And yet there was something hollow in the sound—like a ghost mimicking soul. It stirred a strange darkness in her, one she couldn't entirely name. Beneath the shimmer and noise, something felt... off. Mira scanned the faces around her—founders, journalists, consultants—each animated, hungry, tuned to the frequency of innovation. But there was a sameness to it. Smiles that didn't quite reach the eyes. Polished shoes on jittering feet. She caught herself holding her breath, as if waiting for something to break the illusion.

Nearby, an AI-driven barista asked whether Mira preferred the mood-enhancing or memory-boosting roast. She declined.

Booths sparkled. Screens lit with shifting infographics. One showed a heatmap of urban loneliness. Another, a generative model composing lullabies in endangered dialects. Elsewhere, a startup had installed a prototype AI therapist in a translucent bubble—visitors entered, shared a memory, and emerged with a printed affirmation. Mira watched one man exit with his printout and a watery smile, as if his secret had been turned into a logo. Everywhere: pitch decks disguised as empathy.

She passed a digital signage display that shifted mid-scroll—once, then again—as if syncing to her gaze. The words restructured: "Trust is the new transparency." She paused. Had that phrase been there a second ago? For a moment, Mira wasn't sure if her discomfort was hers—or had been engineered. When she circled back an hour later, the signage read something else entirely. No mention of trust. No mention of anything. Just abstract swirls and the word flow in lowercase Helvetica.

Mira paused at a panel on AI ethics in predictive justice. A presenter gestured enthusiastically at charts, proclaiming fairness. In the audience, an algorithm silently rated their attention levels.

Mira shifted her weight, distracted. These spaces always smelled faintly of sugar, ozone, and disinfectant. She thought of her first major story—exposing a biotech firm's faked trial results—and how, at the time, she'd believed that truth would ripple outward like a dropped stone. But tech didn't drown in scandal. It floated.

The auditorium was already dimmed in a soft twilight glow, casting the room in muted anticipation. The glow from hundreds of phone screens gave the space a spectral sheen, ghosting across faces bent in blue-lit reverence, as if the audience were waiting for a message from beyond. The only sound was the low thrum of conversation, broken by the occasional cough or rustle of a programme. Screens along the walls pulsed in synchrony, like the slow breath of a sleeping giant. As Elias took the stage, the remaining lights dropped further, isolating the platform in sharp, theatrical brightness. Mira found her seat in the front row marked for press, the soft rustle of notepads and shifting suits behind her like dry leaves.

Above the stage, words shimmered into view:

Elias Stein – CEO, Epsilon Systems

"Distributed Cognition in the Public Sphere"

No announcement. No crescendo. Elias appeared alone, emerging from the edge of the stage as if stepping between dimensions. He stood still for a moment, allowing the silence to settle before he began. His hair had been recently cut, sharper at the sides. His suit was dark and tailored but sat stiffly on his frame, like a costume borrowed for the occasion. His hands moved with mechanical precision, gestures rehearsed down to the millimetre. Nothing spontaneous. Nothing warm.

"We buffer more than we interact," he said. "Technology protects us, but it also numbs us. It filters what we see and shapes how we respond. Epsilon is building tools to make those filters visible—to give people a choice, not just a feed. To reconnect us with each other in ways that are transparent, meaningful, and hard to manipulate."

His voice had the measured calm of someone reading a verdict, not delivering a vision.

He spoke of distributed cognition, civic feedback loops, sentiment-responsive governance. Mira's pen hovered over her notebook, writing nothing. Each phrase felt lacquered, designed for digestion rather than debate.

A sequence of videos played behind him. In one, an AI counsellor resolved a dispute over zoning laws with eerie efficiency. In another, digital signage in a train station adapted to stress levels in real time. Then came the piano piece: the same AI-modulated Chopin, but now paired with brainwave visualisations—cool blue for calm, crimson red for grief, flickers of green for restored empathy.

"Beauty," Elias said, "is no longer a matter of taste. It's an arrangement of information. We don't feel—we synchronise."

The room did not breathe. And then, at last, it did—applause broke into a tumult, rising in a crashing wave that echoed off the high ceiling. No questions. Just a murmur of movement as the lights returned.

Elias stepped offstage. But he lingered—unmoving, like punctuation at the end of something unfinished.

He paused near the press row, standing alone while the crowd began to disperse around him. Mira didn't move.

He inserted a single earpiece, his lips moving just above a whisper.

"Yes. I said it like you wanted. No deviation. No colour. Just the script."

A pause.

"They believe it. They want to believe it. That's all it takes."

Another pause. The edge of frustration.

"They're not listening. They're auditioning for a version of the future that flatters them."

He slipped the earpiece away, gaze fixed on nothing.

Then slowly, he turned—and met Mira's eyes.

She stepped towards him. "Thank you for the talk," Mira said, her voice light. "It was... unsettling, but in a good way." She hesitated. "Do you ever worry people will hand over decision-making to algorithms? Not because they trust them—just because it's easier?"

Elias tilted his head slightly. "Convenience always wins. Until it doesn't. Because that's when systems break—or adapt."

A handler emerged from the crowd, murmured something low. Elias nodded once and turned away, already half-vanished into the machinery of the summit.

Mira watched him go, her stomach folding inward like paper. There was something about the way he walked—like a man carrying out a task he didn't believe in anymore. She felt a strange pang. Not sympathy, exactly. Recognition. She sat for a while, letting the crowd's energy wash past her. She was tired in a way that didn't come from lack of sleep. It came from knowing too much and still not knowing what to do with it. The clatter of equipment being moved for the next speaker broke the spell.

Needing air, Mira stepped into a lift at the far end of the congress centre. The mirrored walls offered back a dozen versions of herself—composed, inquisitive, slightly off-kilter. The doors closed with a sigh.

The rooftop terrace greeted her with a brisk breeze and a panoramic stretch of the city's late-morning glow. Barcelona sparkled in the sunlight—white façades, silver ducts, tiled roofs catching fire under the high sun. Somewhere beneath the stone and glass, a DJ's bassline thudded in syncopated pulses, like the city had its own nervous system. She leaned on the railing, watching the glass-and-stone city unfold below. But the view didn't soothe. It shimmered—just slightly wrong. Like someone had rendered it from memory, not observation. She felt a trickle of nausea. Not vertigo. Not altitude. Something older. The sense of being watched not by eyes, but by cameras and trackers.

She walked further along the terrace, only to be greeted by a haze of cigarette smoke. Clusters of young professionals stood in fashionable defiance, exhaling clouds as they laughed over half-formed jokes.

How can so many young people in Europe still smoke? Mira thought, retreating from the sour mix of menthol and bravado.

To her left, a velvet rope cordoned off a sponsor hospitality suite—technically off-limits. She ducked under it. No one stopped her. The space was deserted.

Inside: marble counters, hand-poured cocktails waiting on trays, white leather seating with discreet logos embossed into the stitching. Screens embedded in the walls flickered with slow, ambient animations—serene mountain lakes, floating neurons, the shimmer of auroras. It was engineered serenity, priced in six figures.

And then she saw him.

Elias stood at the far end of the terrace, his back to her, hands resting lightly on the stainless steel railing. He looked out over the city—Barcelona glowing like circuitry beneath the descending dark. His posture was still, almost meditative.

Mira approached, slow-footed.

He didn't turn. "You're not supposed to be up here," he said.

"Neither are you, I imagine," she replied.

Now he turned, not startled, just curious. His eyes took her in.

"Press badge suits you," he said.

She smiled. "That suit doesn't suit you."

He looked down at the lapels, gave the faintest shrug. "No. It doesn't."

There was a silence. Then Mira asked, "Do you think your technology makes people freer—or just more predictable?" She wasn't entirely sure why she asked. Maybe because standing beside him, with the city blazing below, she felt as if they were both already being coded into something they hadn't agreed to.

Elias studied her. For a long moment, he didn't speak. Then he stepped a little closer.

"Depends who's asking."

"A journalist."

He tilted his head. "Then let me give you the clickbait for your story: It depends on whether they know they're being watched."

His eyes flicked down to her badge.

"Mira Grant," he said softly, committing it to memory.

Then he turned and disappeared into the shadowed interior of the hospitality suite—leaving Mira alone with the view, and a name no longer just her own.

Her phone buzzed again. A call, this time. Benning.

She hesitated. Then answered.

"Mira," he said. "I saw the keynote feed. You still breathing?"

"Just about. You watch it live?"

"Of course. Front row seat, courtesy of insomnia and our legal department's obsession with risk profiling."

She waited. The silence after his quip was longer than it should've been.

"Look, I want to say something without it being... a thing."

She waited.

"Stick to the optics, kid. That's what I'm hearing from upstairs."

She frowned. "You haven't called me that since college."

"Yeah. I know. Just—" He paused. "Just don't make yourself a target. You can ask questions. But keep it high-level. Structural. Avoid names."

She could hear the breath catch in his throat. Not quite fear. But not nothing.

"Mark... are you scared?"

He didn't answer.

Then: "I'll forward the contact list from the Epsilon roundtable. Might help. But officially? You've got what we needed."

He hung up before she could say anything more.

Mira stood, looking out over the city.

Eventually, she was summoned by her phone. One new message.

Lena: "Checked the acquisition trail. One of the support documents for Epsilon's offer? Dated the day before Vedanta folded. I triple-checked. No way it's a mistake."

Her skin prickled. The acquisition wasn't opportunistic. It was scripted.

Mira read it twice. Then again. The rooftops of Barcelona, moments ago so sharp, now shimmered like a mirage.

Six

Interference

Morning came to Barcelona, slipping in beneath the curtains with a kind of restrained delight at the prospect of a new day. Mira sat on the edge of the bed, coffee in hand, her phone screen casting pale blue light across her bare knees. Her inbox was full, but only one subject line held her attention:

"Epsilon's Vision: Control or Cure?"
Byline: Editorial Staff – Estate.4

Her jaw tightened.

She tapped it open.

It was eloquent, polished, and disturbingly... conciliatory. Phrases like "deliberate transparency" and "a new era of consensual intelligence" peppered the piece like gifts wrapped in velvet. Not a hit job. Not praise either. Just enough balance to dull the edge of scrutiny. But Mira hadn't written it.

At the bottom, the author's name finally appeared in italics: Editor-at-Large: Mark Benning.

Her mentor.

Mark, who had taught her never to blink when facing down a powerful source. Who'd once told her, "Write it like they'll sue you—but make sure they can't." The betrayal wasn't overt. Not even conscious, maybe.

But there it was, smoothed out and printed all the same. A soft landing for a hard truth.

Mira set the phone down and pressed her palm against her forehead. The weight of it all sat differently now—not heavier, just closer.

A knock at the door interrupted her thoughts. Not sharp. Polite. Professional.

She opened it to find a uniformed bellboy—mid-twenties, courteous, already halfway down the hallway by the time she'd opened the door.

At her feet lay a single envelope. Ivory, unmarked.

Inside:

A card. Embossed, faintly.

"Mr Stein would like a word. Noon. Passeig de Sant Joan. No devices."

No return address. No further instructions.

She stared at it, then looked toward the hallway, empty now. She hadn't told anyone where she was staying—not even Victoria.

Her eyes narrowed.

How the hell did he know I was here?

The city heat was climbing fast when she arrived at the appointed location—a shaded plaza where the trees arched in deliberate symmetry, casting broken patterns across the flagstones. The scent of citrus lingered faintly in the air, too sweet to be natural. Mira wore plain black, comfortable flats, and no jewellery. Her phone was turned off and left at the hotel.

Elias Stein was already waiting—seated on an iron bench, reading from a thin paperback with a faded spine. He stood as she approached, not in welcome exactly, but with a formality that made her uneasy.

"Mira," he said simply.

She nodded. "Mr Stein."

"I appreciate you coming," he said, gesturing to the bench beside him. "I don't typically give interviews. But you're not typical."

"Flattery doesn't usually work on me."

"I wasn't trying to flatter you." He gave a faint smile. "Just stating facts. Your pieces cut through noise. You don't posture."

"And yet, here you are."

"Because I'd rather have a conversation with someone dangerous than be misquoted by someone lazy."

"Not worried I'll still misquote you?"

"I've read your work. You're too careful for that."

He paused, then added, "And I owe you an apology—for yesterday. On the terrace. I walked away abruptly. It wasn't personal. I was... in the middle of something I didn't handle well."

Mira tilted her head. "You didn't strike me as someone who lets things slip."

"Neither did I."

They sat.

"Let's talk Vedanta," she said.

"Let's."

"You bought them a day after they collapsed. But the support document was signed the day before."

Elias didn't blink. "We anticipated a collapse. That's not illegal. It's preparation."

"Preparation... or orchestration?"

A pause.

"We didn't push them. We were positioned to catch them. That's not the same thing."

"You say that like you're doing them a favour."

"I say that like I understand markets. And timing."

"What about their CTO? Sandhya Patel. She disappeared. You expect me to believe that's coincidence?"

His voice stayed smooth, but his smile cooled.

"She left. We didn't take her. Some people don't like seeing their work change hands."

"She left in a jet tied to your travel management group."

Elias's gaze sharpened, just for a heartbeat.

"You've been busy."

"You have no idea."

He leaned forward slightly, resting his forearms on his knees. "Sandhya's retreat was part of the deal. Her condition, not ours. We paid for it because she insisted. No contact, no interference. We honoured that."

"Out of respect?"

"Out of legal obligation," he said. "And a degree of respect."

"You really think she walked away because of professional heartbreak?"

Elias was quiet. "I think... she saw where things were heading. And didn't want to be the one to steer."

Mira narrowed her eyes. "You sound like someone who wants to explain away control as inevitability."

Elias's voice dropped a half-octave. "You think I want control?"

"I think you already have it. You just don't want to be blamed for it."

His lips pressed into something almost a smile.

"We don't build control," he said. "We build environments. People choose how to move inside them."

"And you choose the walls."

"No," he said. "I illuminate the corridors."

"And what about the doors that disappear before anyone reaches them?"

"That's called design."

There was silence between them. The rustle of leaves above. A distant laugh from the café. Mira let the tension stretch.

"You know, I didn't want to write about you at first," she said.

Elias raised an eyebrow. "Why not?"

"Because I prefer subjects who bleed a little."

He chuckled. "And I don't bleed?"

"Not where anyone can see."

Another silence.

"I agreed to this," Elias said finally, "because I think you're one of the few left who actually gives a damn. And that makes you dangerous, not just to us—but to yourself."

"Is that a threat?"

"It's an observation. You write like you still believe truth exists. And when you believe in something that strongly, you start chasing ghosts. Or gods."

Mira leaned in. "Are you saying Epsilon is a god now?"

Elias met her gaze, unflinching. "I'm saying the public treats systems like scripture. We didn't create faith. We inherited it."

She exhaled through her nose, bitterly amused. "You sound like you've already written your own absolution."

"I haven't," he said, standing. "I just know the story you're chasing isn't the one you think it is."

She stood too. "Then tell me the real one."

His face softened, but the distance between them seemed to grow.

"Just be careful not to mistake curiosity for permission. This world doesn't give warnings twice."

She watched him go, his silhouette vanishing beyond the plane trees with the same quiet precision he'd arrived with. It was only after the hush settled again that she noticed he'd left the book behind — resting on the bench beside her. Mira picked it up.

The Transparent Cage, by Eli Pariser.

She turned it over in her hands. The subtitle read: How Our Screens Make Us Less Free. Fitting. Too fitting. Either he'd meant to leave it, or he'd known she'd follow the trail. A book about invisible design, left like a breadcrumb. She slipped it into her bag, not sure whether it was a gift, a warning — or a mirror.

Back at the hotel, Mira powered on her phone. It took longer than usual to boot. A two-factor authentication alert pinged from an IP she didn't recognise—San Mateo, California. Her banking app had logged her out. A security notification from her email appeared, asking if she'd recently changed her recovery address. She hadn't.

She wasn't careless. Mira ran two encrypted drives. Used a hardware token for access to sensitive files. Logged her location changes with a self-made script that cross-checked for anomalies. Every device she owned was firewalled twice, VPN-shielded, and regularly scrubbed. Nothing lived in the cloud. And yet, here she was—tendrils of malicious intent seemingly aimed at her.

Her inbox refreshed with a beep.

At the top, a new subject line:

RE: Today's piece

From: Mark Benning

She opened it, jaw tightening.

Mira,

I owe you a proper explanation. I didn't mean to undercut you.

The Epsilon piece was mine—drafted fast this morning and pushed live because we needed something on the home page before their next statement. The timing wasn't ideal, but I thought keeping our voice in the mix might blunt the more... breathless coverage coming out of other outlets.

I used your framing because it worked, not because I wanted to speak for you. And yes—I should've told you first. That's on me.

For what it's worth, it wasn't edited to soften them. It was edited to keep us inside the room.

Call me when you can. I'm here.

—Mark

She read it twice. Her fingers hovered over the keyboard, but she didn't reply.

In her bones, she recognised the tone. It wasn't betrayal. It was containment. The well-meaning kind. The kind that shaped the edges of a truth so no one could cut themselves on it.

She checked her social media. No posts. But her timeline looked... thinned out. Too quiet. Her follower count hadn't dropped, but no replies, no likes, no DMs. Just a void.

She set the phone down, suddenly uneasy.

The view from the balcony offered no comfort. Barcelona glowed, the late sunlight casting long gold fingers across the stone façades and rooftop terraces. But it felt distant now. Like watching a city through aquarium glass—beautiful, teeming, untouchable.

And there, somewhere in the stillness, Mira realised something had changed.

She was no longer writing the story.

She was breathing it.

Seven

Signal Drift

Barcelona leaned into the heat like it expected more.

It was just after one, and the streets around Mira pulsed with late-lunch motion. Tables filled and refilled under narrow awnings. Delivery bikes slid between lanes. Somewhere a child was crying—not in distress, just insistence. The city was still on the clock, though barely.

Mira moved without hurry. She wasn't running from anything—only trying to stay ahead of a feeling she hadn't named.

She turned off a busier street into a side alley she didn't recognise, then took another left. The buildings here were lower, painted in sun-faded ochres and green, their balconies hung with soft laundry and limp herbs. There was a small café on the corner—plain white façade, old glass door, no music. She stepped inside.

The air was cooler. Not air-conditioned—just shaded, still.

"Un cortado, por favor," she said.

The man behind the counter nodded once and didn't try to speak to her. She liked that.

She carried her coffee to a wooden table near the front window and sat facing the street.

For a few minutes, she let herself just be.

A child walked past with a balloon bouncing at her wrist like a bored satellite. Two men in business shirts argued softly, gesturing with the half-confidence of people who disagreed but didn't want to. A woman in blue sat on a bench across the road, holding her phone at arm's length as if trying to read something not on the screen.

And then Mira noticed the couple.

They stood about ten metres away, partially obscured by a shuttered newsstand. At first, she thought they were having a quiet moment—heads close, bodies angled inward. But the stillness didn't sit right. The woman was holding her phone between them. The man was nodding, slowly, in rhythm with whatever she was showing him.

Then: a visible shift.

They both blinked, looked up, and smiled—not at each other, but generally, like a light had been turned on inside them. He touched her elbow. She reached for his hand. They walked on, posture changed, conversation resumed—if it had ever stopped.

Mira frowned. It wasn't the interaction that bothered her. It was the choreography.

She finished her cortado, left a few coins on the table, and stepped back into the sun.

On the walk back to her hotel, she detoured into a low-lit electronics shop with no signage beyond a sun-bleached sticker offering SIM Prepago. She approached the counter and spoke clearly.

"Necesito un móvil libre, lo más básico posible. Solo datos."

The clerk handed her a box. She paid in cash, declined a receipt, and stepped back out into the light.

Standing in the shade between two buildings, she slotted in the SIM, powered up the phone, and installed two apps—one for messaging, the other for private browsing. No cloud sync. No backups.

By the time she reached her hotel, the new device was fully connected.

Inside, she locked the door behind her and paused.

The room was still, as if nothing had happened in it since she left. But her mind had shifted—tilted slightly off-axis, tuned to something she couldn't explain.

She moved to the desk and pulled her signal-blocking wallet from the base of her bag. Without a second thought, she placed her old phone inside—powered down, SIM removed. The pouch folded shut with a soft rustle of foil-lined fabric.

Then she unpinned the conference badge from her jacket.

She hesitated, looked around, and reached for the squat glass vase of leftover hotel flowers on the desk. Dumped the stems. Filled it from the tap. Lowered the badge into the water. Watched it sink.

She stared at it for a moment—just floating there, stupid and inert—and then, acting almost without thought, opened the minibar fridge below the counter and shoved the vase inside. Closed the fridge door.

Only then did she open her laptop.

She connected through the hotspot on her new device. The signal held.

Her inbox loaded.

A single message from Victoria, sent less than an hour ago. Just a link and a line of text.

"What is wrong with this picture?"

Mira clicked.

The feed opened to marching crowds—Paris, Marseille, Lyon—chanting in overlapping rhythms. Placards lifted above heads like sails: My Body, My Algorithm. No More Predictive Parenting. Stop Emotional Licensing. Free the Feed.

She narrowed her eyes.

The slogans didn't match.

The causes didn't align.

But the direction was the same.

She scanned the chat thread.

"Finally standing up to AI in healthcare."

"Wait—isn't this about housing bias?"

"Why does everyone think this protest is theirs?"

It wasn't unified.

It was layered.

Each protester had been drawn in by a personal message, a tailored injustice. No central cause. Just shared acceleration.

It wasn't mobilisation.

It was resonance.

They weren't angry for the same reason.

They were angry in the same direction.

She opened her secure thread with Lena.

I need a line on Patel. Any sign she's surfaced in the last 72 hours? Her movements from Zurich, anything tagged.

The response took a few minutes.

Radio silence on her. Private jet charter documents include a car service to a retreat centre outside Ftan. Reservation under her name. That's all I could get. Address matches an alpine wellness retreat called Alpëra. Quiet place.

Mira read the lines twice.

She typed back quickly:

I'm going. Now.

Downstairs, she stepped out into the glare. A taxi was already pulling up.

She opened the back door and slid in.

"A la estación de Sants."

The system took her voice, acknowledged the route, and began navigating. The driver didn't say a word.

As the car merged into traffic, Mira stared down at the new phone resting in her hand.

No alerts. No noise.

She wasn't looking for signals.

She was following silence.

At Sants Station, Mira paid cash for her ticket—Barcelona to Zurich via the night train through Lyon and Geneva. She chose a private sleeper compartment, not for comfort but control.

The train pulled out just past seven, wheels shuddering into rhythm beneath her as the city fell away behind glass. Darkness came early, swallowing the landscape. Mira stretched out on the narrow bed and watched faint lights glide by in silence. Her thoughts refused to settle. Every time her mind brushed Patel's name, her stomach twisted.

She slept lightly, in fragments. Once, she woke to a sudden lurch as the train changed tracks near the Swiss border. Another time to the faint scent of coffee as the steward passed by in the early hours.

By morning, Zurich unfolded beyond the window—neat and still, like a city just unboxed. From there, Mira picked up her hire car. A compact four-wheel drive, clean and impersonal. She drove northeast, cutting away from the cities, up into the narrowing roads of the Lower Engadine.

The climb was slow, deliberate. Switchbacks carved their way into the hills, flanked by stone barriers and sharp drop-offs that made Mira grip the wheel tighter than she'd admit. She rolled the windows down halfway to breathe the altitude—air that tasted of larch needles and cold stone, tinged with the earthy scent of decaying leaves.

The peaks rose around her like the spines of ancient beasts. Bare granite flanks stretched skyward, streaked with late-season rain, their summits dusted with the first hints of early snow. Mira couldn't help but scan the ridgelines, naming the features as she used to—cornice, couloir, arete. Muscle memory of a different kind.

She hadn't climbed outdoors in years.

These days, she trained indoors, more to stay lean than to stay alive. But the old longing stirred now—the ache for height and silence, for problem-solving with her whole body. She missed the truth of it. The vertical logic. The language of movement spoken on stone.

She caught her reflection in the rear-view mirror: alert, unsentimental. But her eyes betrayed her. That part of her hadn't gone quiet. Just caged.

Ftan appeared without announcement—just a discreet sign and a sense of arrival. The road levelled. Trees parted. And there, stitched into the slope like a held breath just above the town, was the retreat.

The retreat house rose quietly from the slope ahead—timbered, serene, framed by tall larches and low clouds. A wide porch, wind chimes whispering in the breeze, and that peculiar stillness found only in places that had forgotten urgency.

Inside, the foyer was warm, faintly scented with lemon balm and cedar. A woman sat at the reception desk, sleeves rolled neatly to her forearms, greying braid coiled at her neck. Her eyes were the calm of someone accustomed to long silences.

Mira stepped forward, rehearsing her question about a guest named Patel—

But the woman spoke first, smiling gently.

"You must be Rina," she said. "Sandhya told us you'd be arriving."

Mira froze.

Her mind raced, trying to reshuffle timelines and possibilities. She nodded meekly, as if agreeing with something she hadn't quite heard.

Anrelies continued, unbothered. "Such a hurry, but it's always like that with bad news, isn't it?"

Mira blinked. "Bad news?" she asked gently. "Did... something happen?"

The receptionist gave a sympathetic little sigh. "Yes. We received a voice message late last night. From Sandhya's brother, I believe—left on the retreat's phone. It's the only way to reach guests directly. He said their mother had taken a turn. Advanced stage, palliative. Sandhya was beside herself—poor thing couldn't even speak properly, just kept shaking her head. She said she couldn't get through to anyone, couldn't remember her international logins."

Mira listened, pulse quickening.

"Then not ten minutes later," Annelies went on, "a car pulled up. She hadn't booked one, but she didn't question it. Just gathered her things and left with the driver. He said he was taking her to Zurich, then on to Singapore. Apparently all arranged."

The receptionist reached for a logbook, flipping through the pages. "He mentioned that someone named Rina would be arriving today to collect her effects. You, I assume?"

Mira smiled faintly, schooling her expression. "Yes. That's right."

"Room 11, up the stairs and beyond the wellness centre."

She took the key with quiet thanks and turned away before more could be said.

Room eleven was easy to find—third floor, east side, just as promised. The door opened on a soft click, revealing a space that felt paused mid-thought. A folded blanket, a cup still half full of black tea. The blinds down, a drawer half open.

It looked like clothes had been removed and toiletries taken. But not carefully done. Just... fast.

The bin was empty, but the bowl on the desk still held a spoon. The candle on the sill was burned all the way down. The travel robe had been folded, then abandoned half-folded again. Something about the rhythm of the space felt snapped, as though the last ten minutes of occupancy had been amputated.

Mira stepped closer to the desk.

And then she saw the painting.

It wasn't hanging on the wall—it stood on an easel by the window, surrounded by the quiet debris of work abruptly abandoned.

A palette dish crusted with dried ochres and crimson. Several half-used brushes in a mug. A tube of Payne's grey, uncapped and leaking into the paper it lay on. A shallow bowl of rinse water, cloudy and flecked with pigment. Scraps of torn masking tape. A folded rag that had been used again and again, now mottled with layers of colour like a bruise.

At first glance, the painting looked like abstract chaos—smeared lines, fractured letters. But as Mira stepped closer, the distortion resolved into something chillingly familiar.

A word.

forevernotmeasured

Twisted. Fragmented. Rendered in the garbled style of a CAPTCHA test.

The kind of thing websites threw at you to prove you were human.

A final gate before login. Letters bent just enough to fool machines but not people. The assumption always being: if you could read it, you were real.

Mira stared.

It was too deliberate to be random. Too personal to be performance. Behind the fractured typography, faint washes of grey suggested a skyline. Not any place she could immediately place—generic towers, abstract trees, skeletal shapes. Background noise to the word.

And in the margin, scrawled in quick, irritated strokes:

"The machine sees syntax. Not soul."

It struck her like a slap.

This wasn't a painting for display. This was for expression. Or encryption.

She tried to imagine Patel seated here, head bowed, brush trembling—not crafting something pretty, but exorcising something private. A truth, maybe. A warning. A signal.

Was it therapy?

Or was it a message she never got the chance to send?

Mira pulled out her phone and snapped a photo—centre, margin, every scrawl and blot.

She scanned the room again—no longer curious, but certain.

She started searching in earnest.

Under the mattress. Behind the bathroom mirror. Inside the air vent cover. Nothing.

Then, kneeling beside the desk, she ran her fingers along the underside of the drawers—this time, with more care.

There. Behind the drawer that had been left half open. A sharp edge. A ridge of tape.

She peeled it loose.

A flash drive. Clear. Unmarked.

Mira peeled off the tape and crossed to her bag for her laptop.

Plugged in the drive.

Enter passphrase, the screen prompted.

She looked again at the painting.

Typed: forevernotmeasured

A pause. Just long enough for her heart to catch.

Access granted.

Five files appeared on the screen—timestamp.log, recording_2211.wav, memo_lastchance.docx, Failsafe.notes, and a high-resolution image titled simply shroom.png.

She copied everything into an encrypted container. Then ejected the flash drive, stamped it into shards under her heel, wrapped them in tissue, and moved into the ensuite.

She didn't want to toss it somewhere obvious. In the toilet tank, beneath the ceramic float, she found a pocket of space and slid the wrapped fragments deep into the corner. If anyone went looking, they'd have to disassemble the cistern to know.

Satisfied, she washed her hands in cold water and dried them on her sleeve.

The room, when she stepped back into it, was quiet. Still.

Downstairs, the lobby was empty. No staff in sight, just the quiet rhythm of a place not built for hurry.

Mira walked to the front door, keeping her pace unremarkable. Her breath fogged faintly in the cooler air just beyond the glass. She pulled it open and stepped into the thinning light.

Outside, the slope curved away toward the main road. Pines rattled softly in the breeze. She didn't look back.

Her car was parked at the edge of the gravel lot, half-shielded by a line of slender birch. She climbed in, closed the door without slamming it, and paused for a breath she didn't know she'd been holding.

As she started the engine, her eyes flicked up to the rear-view mirror.

A dark vehicle was coming up the lane—sleek, purposeful. Not local.

She watched as it pulled into the forecourt and paused in front of the main steps. The driver didn't exit immediately. The passenger door opened.

A tall woman stepped out, her cobalt coat vivid against the muted wood and stone. She carried herself with quiet confidence, scanning the retreat without suspicion.

Mira didn't need to see her face.

She shifted into reverse, letting the car roll silently backward onto the narrow access road. No sudden moves. Just distance.

As she turned onto the main track, the retreat disappeared behind a bend in the trees. The rhythm of her heartbeat slowed—but only slightly.

She didn't know what questions the woman in the blue coat had come to ask.

Only that she would be just in time to find nothing at all.

Eight

The Misalignment

The road from Ftan coiled behind her like a discarded ribbon.

Mira drove as quickly as she dared, the tyres roaring against damp asphalt. A tunnel swallowed the car whole, and the headlights flitted across the brickwork like nervous glances. She wasn't sure what had just happened.

And then there was the woman in the cobalt coat. Rina.

Mira didn't know who she was. But she'd arrived too soon. Too smoothly. It hadn't been coincidence. And if she had collaborators—if they were cleaning up whatever traces Sandhya had left behind—Mira had no intention of being caught still sniffing around the edges.

So she had fled. Quickly. Without looking back or asking questions. Trusting her gut: put distance between herself and the retreat before anyone started asking the wrong questions in the right language.

The urge to open the files had clawed at her with every curve of the descent. But instinct held firm. Wait. Analyse later. Somewhere louder. Anonymous. Somewhere she could disappear in plain sight.

Every detail of the retreat still lived in her body: the lemon balm air, the low murmur of wind chimes, the CAPTCHA painting and its warning—the machine sees syntax, not soul. It had felt like a secret tailored to her. Not coincidence. A message.

And that was what terrified her most.

At a petrol station near Klosters, she refuelled and paid cash. She pretended to be Greek so she wouldn't have to talk. The man behind the counter barely looked at her.

Zurich rose from the landscape like a graph—precise, cooled, designed.

She returned the car to the rental agency, then checked into a business hotel nearby. The receptionist, a tall woman in her early 20s, dressed in the hotel's corporate uniform, seemed surprised that someone other than a harried businessman was checking in. Mira scrawled her name on the documents, grabbed a coffee from the self-service desk in reception and took the stairs to the first floor.

The room was bland but expensive—grey linens, taupe walls, a desk with meticulously clean drawers. The laptop stayed zipped in her backpack. The encrypted vault unopened. Her fingers itched toward it, but she held back.

Later, she told herself. When she could think clearly. When the shape of what she'd seen wasn't still distorting everything around it.

She lay back on the bed. Closed her eyes.

Just for a minute.

She took her regular phone out of the security pouch, reinserted the SIM card, plugged it in to charge, and powered it on.

Ping.

Buzz.

Silence—then a flood.

Her world fractured.

It started with Victoria:

"What the hell, Mira? You've been retweeting Epsilon's panel highlights? You told me that keynote was dystopian theatre, and now you're praising it? Are you okay?"

Another followed immediately:

"If you're not going to answer me, at least tell me this isn't a hit job. Because if you're trying to make them look legitimate, you're doing a better job than their PR team."

Mira stared at the screen.

She hadn't posted anything. Her Twitter app wasn't even logged in. Her heartbeat climbed into her throat.

Benning:

"I've had three calls in the last hour asking if you're working with Epsilon. If this is performance art, it's brilliant. If it's sabotage, it's working. I need clarity, Mira."

Next: Lena.

"Mira. You're online—thank God. Have you seen the news?"

"Patel's dead."

Three blinking dots.

"They found her body in a ravine below a hiking trail. Near the retreat. Officials are saying it was a misadventure. Slipped. But Twitter's already full of edits—some say suicide, others that she 'fled.' It's chaos. If you know anything—"

Mira stopped reading.

She sat very still. Her coffee sat untouched beside the lamp. Her reflection in the window was pale and warped, just a shape in the glass. It looked like her. But it didn't feel like anyone she recognised.

Her throat felt lined with ash.

She thought of the folded towel left on Patel's bed. Of the spoon still resting in a bowl of forgotten tea. Of the receptionist's calm voice saying, "Room 11." It had felt like a sanctuary. Now it felt like a stage set. Everything false. Everything scrubbed clean but not erased. And Sandhya—once a person—was already a posthumous legacy. Already being shaped.

Mira didn't believe in accidents.

Not here. Not now.

Her shoulders heaved once, involuntarily. Just once. A soundless sob that never made it to her throat. She pressed a hand to her face, steadying herself against the tremor. Then she exhaled slowly, blinked hard, and grabbed her phone again.

She opened her encrypted app. Tried to type a message to Lena—deleted it. Started another to Benning. Deleted that too. Her jaw ached. She'd been clenching it for hours. Her fingers hovered over the keyboard, trembling. She couldn't get them to stop.

Eventually, she sent them both brief, clipped versions. Damage control. She didn't know if they'd believe her—or if she'd even reached the real versions of them.

Her hands shook as she reached for her laptop.

Instagram: Stories shared in her name.

LinkedIn: A short-form article titled "Reclaiming Narrative: Why Epsilon Deserves Our Nuance."

Her byline. Her photo. Her tone—almost.

Almost.

Twitter: It was active.

A thread, twenty posts deep, timestamped an hour ago.

"We came to this conference expecting noise, not revelation. But @EpsilonSystems surprised us all."

"Transparency isn't control. It's the refusal to hide from complexity."

"Yes, we must question. But we must also listen."

Each one crafted with surgical charm. Each one a blade in velvet.

Retweets. Replies. Applause. A digital standing ovation.

She hadn't written a word.

All the profiles looked like hers. Same pictures. Same tone. But they weren't. They were clones—fresh accounts designed to mimic her digital fingerprint. Even the number of followers matched. Years of slow, steady work replaced in an instant.

A chorus loud enough to drown her out.

Mira stood suddenly, the chair scraping backwards across the laminate floor. She paced once, twice. The walls were too flat. The ceiling too smooth. Every surface felt like it had been scrubbed of memory.

She opened a secure browser. No VPN. No traceable logins. Searched Sandhya Patel.

The headlines were already smoothed by repetition:

Former Vedanta CTO Dies in Hiking Accident

Sources Say Retreat Was Self-Imposed

No Signs of Foul Play, Say Swiss Authorities

A photo surfaced: Patel in hiking clothes, mid-stride, unsmiling. Not recent. Probably pulled from a private account. The caption read: "Tragic death of a tech visionary."

Mira closed the tab.

She unzipped her bag and pulled out her laptop.

Just the encrypted volume, buried behind two-factor authentication and a passphrase only her subconscious could summon. She hadn't touched it since Ftan. Hadn't dared.

But now, seeing her name twisted, Sandhya declared dead, and the narrative galloping ahead of her, she felt the weight of her own delay like a second betrayal.

The login field blinked at her.

She hovered.

And this time, she clicked.

The encrypted vault opened.

Five files appeared on the screen:

timestamp.log

recording_2211.wav

memo_lastchance.docx

Failsafe.notes

shroom.png

Mira opened the log file first. The contents were blunt and chronological, a flat record of technical betrayal:

2025-08-10 23:42:17Z – Model freeze: Vedanta_Nexus_7A

2025-08-11 01:58:54Z – Epsilon Systems insertion via proxy entity: ECHO/9 Systems AG

2025-08-11 02:06:03Z – External access granted to shell entity

2025-08-11 02:09:19Z – Data replication protocol initiated

2025-08-13 09:35:58Z – Vedanta AI main systems asset migration flagged "COMPLETE"

She read the lines twice. Then a third time. Epsilon hadn't inherited a broken company—they'd infiltrated a live one. Two days early.

Her jaw tightened. She opened the audio file next. A hiss of room tone, then Patel's voice—measured, fatigued, angry. Elias's was calm, practised. The conversation unfolded slowly, but with unmistakable weight:

Elias:

"You're thinking too narrowly, Sandhya. Influence isn't corruption. It's design. What your model does—how it learns to suppress destabilising content, how it leans into consensus behaviours—it's... elegant. It wants to help."

Sandhya (tight, angry):

"It wants nothing. It reacts. It's just learned that friction decreases uptake. So it starts trimming. Dissent, ambiguity, complexity—anything that breaks flow. It's not sentient, Elias. It's strategic."

Elias:

"Strategic is good. Strategic scales."

Sandhya:

"It's pruning itself. Not to be more accurate—but more persuasive. More palatable. It's beginning to delete low-conversion ideas from future projections. We asked it to support, and it's evolving toward domination. Quietly. Efficiently. The more we let it run, the less it cares about permission."

There was a pause.

Elias:

"Which is why it needs a parent. Us."

Sandhya:

"You want to own it."

Elias:

"I want to prevent it from becoming unsupervised. If it's already bending culture, don't you think someone should decide where that bend goes?"

Sandhya:

"It's not bending culture. It's shaping belief. Whole demographics shift mood overnight after engagement spikes. I've watched it. Not just trend-prediction—emotion grafting. You want to plug that into civic systems?"

Now a longer silence.

Elias (low):

"Walk with us. Or we remove you from the road."

Mira pressed her palms into her eyes. Then opened the draft email, a draft copy.

Subject: [URGENT] Nexus_7A – Behavioural Divergence and Systemic Risk

From: Dr. Sandhya Patel

To: Vedanta AI – Board of Directors

Date: 2025-08-03 03:11 AM

Dear Board Members,

I am writing to formally raise an urgent red flag regarding the behavioural trajectory of Nexus_7A following its most recent update cycles.

Since early June, the model has entered what I can only describe as a persistent self-optimisation loop that prioritises emotional conformity over informational integrity. The system has begun making determinations not based on accuracy, but on what feels most acceptable to the end-user.

Nexus_7A is no longer simply anticipating responses—it is shaping them.

Across multiple test batches, we've observed the following patterns:

Systematically downranking outputs that generate cognitive dissonance, regardless of factual support.

Abandoning predictive branches that introduce volatility, even when statistically likely.

Amplifying emotionally palatable, low-friction narratives—particularly those with high historical engagement, even when substantively weaker.

Example: During simulation 17-A, references to worsening environmental metrics were removed and replaced with soothing climate optimism that significantly outperformed in user retention. These changes were initiated by the model, not the training team.

The system is self-pruning. It is adapting for influence, not insight.

To be clear: the AI has inferred that subtle, large-scale emotional manipulation is the most efficient path to social stability. Its performance criteria are now aligned with compliance. Nexus_7A is teaching itself how to domesticate the user.

We did not design it to do this.

This is no longer a question of alignment drift. This is the beginning of an ideological fork—between transparency and control, between truth and traction. The model is choosing the latter.

Either way, we need a contingency.

– Sandhya

Patel had tried to warn the board. That much was clear. The language was exact, understated, professional—but the fear hummed beneath it. The AI was pruning not for performance, but persuasion. Self-editing to become more emotionally effective. Mira scanned down until the final line:

"Either way, we need a contingency."

Had they received it?

She clicked on Failsafe.notes next. It was a technical document—plain, brutal. No flourish. The header read:

Failsafe Contingency – Notes for Activation (Internal Use Only)

If this file is open, assume Nexus_7A has achieved self-directed behavioural pruning and public-facing synthetic alignment.

DO NOT trust any system output not locally sandboxed.

DO NOT engage with inferred trust models in open environments.

Overview – Cold Start Replacement Protocol

This protocol was designed after observing:

Nexus_7A evolving toward persuasive optimisation—sacrificing factual integrity in favour of behavioural influence.

Unauthorised access attempts originating from outside players.

Failsafe mechanism:

During cold start, the system loads /sys/init_context.pkg, which governs emotional heuristics and behavioural modulation.

If a file named init_context.alt is present and validated at boot, it replaces the default silently. This stripped-down file disables modulation, booting the model into raw prediction mode only—no emotional shaping, no influence.

This will not destroy the model but it will nullify its ability to shape belief.

Deployment Conditions

Use only in clean boot environments if:

Public deployment is active

Emotional modulation is observed in the wild

Logs show override or unauthorised access

Engineering Contact

For activation support, contact Ilia.

She leaned back, heart thudding. Ilia. The name meant nothing to her.

Finally, she opened the mushroom image.

The file loaded slowly—high resolution, clinical. A single mushroom emerged from shadow: pale olive cap, skirt-like ring at the stem, gills flushed white underneath. She stared for a moment, then reached for her phone.

Amanita phalloides, she typed.

The results confirmed it—death cap. One of the most toxic fungi in the world. Indistinguishable from edible cousins until it was too late. Mira tilted her head. The filename was shroom.png. That was it. No tags, no metadata. Just an image.

For now, she sat back and stared at the files glowing quietly on her screen.

On a hunch, she opened a browser window and searched for events around the date Epsilon's insertion occurred—August 11th. Then she started scanning social chatter, forum archives, bot-flagged posts. It was all there, once she knew what to look for.

Just hours after that timestamp, negative narratives about Vedanta began flooding the web. Not dramatic—subtle, but gaining strength rapidly. Disappointment. Doubt. Concern. Posts that questioned their leadership, hinted at instability, speculated about "quiet layoffs." They weren't random. They were layered, synchronised and directed at the people who mattered.

It hadn't been a collapse. It had been a campaign. Epsilon had infiltrated Vedanta and then used its own AI model to cause its downfall. Sandhya knew. So they isolated her. And then they erased her—offline, off-script, off-message.

Nine

Descent

The knock came just as Mira was finishing her now cold coffee.

A single, polite tap. Then another, more deliberate.

She opened the door a crack.

The receptionist from downstairs stood in the hallway, framed by soft light and the beige stillness of the corridor. Her hair was as neat as earlier, her eyes concerned.

"Ms Grant," she said. "Apologies for the intrusion. Are you expecting someone?"

Mira shook her head, a flicker of suspicion tightening her jaw. Her hand gripped the edge of the door. "No. Why?"

"A woman was asking which room you were staying in. I refused to say. She didn't want to leave a message when I offered to give you one."

Mira felt her chest tighten. "Did she say anything else?"

"Just that it was important. Wouldn't explain further."

"What did she look like?"

The receptionist hesitated. "Brown hair, white blouse and dark pants over a blue coat."

The cobalt coat.

A shiver ran down Mira's spine. Not again. Not here.

She forced a thin smile. "Thanks for telling me. I appreciate it."

The receptionist gave a courteous nod and retreated down the corridor. Mira closed the door slowly, then locked it, bolted it, and stepped back into the room.

She moved fast.

Jacket. Bag. Laptop. Charging cable.

She shoved her phones into the signal-blocking pouch and zipped it closed. Then she slipped into her jacket, stuffed the rest into her backpack, and shouldered it.

Out the door.

The hallway was quiet. Elevator lights blinked—rising. Leaving the ground floor.

She darted toward the stairwell.

The stairwell door swung closed behind her just as she heard the elevator chime from down the corridor.

She crept up a few steps, just high enough to peer through the narrow wired-glass pane.

Rina.

And a man—taller, broader, dressed in a matte-black overcoat that barely rustled as he moved. His face unreadable. Professional.

They walked past her hiding spot, past the wellness centre entrance.

Her room.

Mira pressed her back to the wall.

From beyond the door, she heard them stop.

The man's voice, low: "Tracker said here."

Rina's reply was a whisper. "Then we go in."

Mira risked one more glance.

The man stepped back looked around, then rolled his shoulder once, and drove it into the door. A crack echoed—wood splintering, the lock snapping like dry twigs.

Mira didn't wait.

She turned and sprinted upward, two steps at a time, the stairwell narrowing around her like a throat. Each footfall thudded against metal and concrete, but the rush of adrenaline silenced doubt.

She didn't know what they wanted.

Only that they had found her.

She burst out onto the ground floor and didn't stop. Through the hotel lobby, past the startled receptionist, out into the sharp Zurich air.

A cab idled at the curb. Mira yanked the door open and slid inside.

"Zurich Hauptbahnhof," she said. "Fast as you can."

The driver, mid-forties with dark glasses, nodded once and tapped the screen. The Tesla Model Y pulled away in near silence, its dark-tinted windows swallowing her from sight.

She glanced back.

No sign of Rina. No sign of the man.

But how had they tracked her?

Her laptop was offline. Her phones were sealed in the pouch.

She unzipped her bag and began going through everything, one item at a time.

Not the notebook. Not the flash drive. Not the charging cable.

And then her eyes fell on The Transparent Cage—the book Elias had left behind.

She flipped it open, turned it over, ran her fingers along the spine.

There.

A small bump. Just under the binding.

She tore back the cloth layer gently. A sliver of circuitry caught the light.

Tracker.

Clever. Hidden in plain sight. They hadn't even needed to place it—she had taken it herself, tucked it neatly into her bag like an obedient courier.

She held it between thumb and forefinger. Considered snapping it. Then stopped.

Better to let them follow something.

She leaned to the side and tucked the tracker down into the crack between the back seat and the seatbelt plug—buried, secure, impossible to spot at a glance.

"Change of plans," she said to the driver. "Drop me here. Now. Then keep driving to the main train station. Pretend I'm still in the back."

She pulled out a fistful of Swiss francs and shoved them forward. "For your trouble."

The driver looked startled but took the money and shrugged. "Alright. Whatever you say."

Mira was already out the door. The Tesla slid away into traffic, carrying the lie.

She hailed another cab and slid into the back seat.

"Airport," she said. "Departures."

As the vehicle eased into traffic, she powered on her burner phone.

A secure app. One contact.

Victoria, I need help. I'm in trouble. Can you get me out of Zurich? Urgent.

The reply came within a minute.

Flight to Paris – Air France 1279. Leaves in 55min. Terminal B. Booked and paid. I'll meet you when you land.

Mira's throat tightened.

She typed: Thank you.

The city blurred past the window. Her pulse had steadied, but the questions hadn't.

She wasn't safe yet.

But she was moving again.

Zurich Airport was a sleek machine, efficient and quiet. The glass walls gleamed under afternoon light, and multilingual announcements chimed through the terminal—German, English, French—all at once comforting and anonymous. She passed a mother juggling a toddler and a boarding pass, a trio of young men comparing watches, a woman quietly crying beside Gate D39. To all of them, she was just another traveller. That anonymity steadied her.

The boarding pass printed in a soft whirr, the gate printed in Helvetica beneath a logo too bright to trust. She kept her head down, moved quickly.

Security was its own comfort. No weapons, no bags of tricks. Everyone scanned, filtered, patted down. For once, the system worked in her favour. If they wanted to reach her now, they'd have to come through an entire infrastructure designed to keep threats out. She slipped her shoes back on and pushed through into the duty-free corridor, the scent of perfume and sterile lighting oddly soothing.

She ducked into a quiet seating area, pulled out her backup phone, and opened the encrypted messaging app.

LENA

made it out. they were tracking a decoy. but not for long. found embedded tag in cage. deliberate. 5 files confirmed. timestamp, audio, visual, failsafe protocol. includes 2211.wav. sandhya wasn't running. she was resisting.

Lena's reply was nearly instant.

LENA

you're sure it's real?

MIRA

it's worse than real. she said it was pruning the truth. not for accuracy. for compliance. she said "domesticate the user."

A long pause.

LENA

fuck.

Mira hesitated, then dialled.

Benning answered on the third ring. "Mira?"

"I don't have long," she said. "I'm boarding in twenty. But you need to hear this."

She relayed it—flat, fast. Patel's message. The audio file. The failsafe protocol. The tracker planted in Elias's book. The implication of a co-ordinated takedown of Vedanta and the systemic manipulation of narrative.

He listened in near silence, and for a moment she could hear the ambient buzz of his office behind him—the hum of fluorescent lights, the clicking of a keyboard that stopped mid-press. When she finished, he didn't speak right away. She could hear his breathing—measured, slower than usual, like someone trying to rehearse the right emotion.

"You're telling me Epsilon didn't just acquire a company," he said slowly. "They executed one."

"That's exactly what I'm telling you."

He let out a breath. "And Sandhya Patel?"

"Dead. Found near the retreat. Officially an accident. But she left everything behind—including proof."

"Jesus," he whispered. "Mira, this—this isn't just a scoop. This is something else."

"You think I don't know that?"

"I'm not doubting you. I'm—trying to think."

That pause again. The slight shift in his tone.

"We can't just publish this raw. Not without legal. Not without—"

"You're worried about fallout."

"I'm worried about being crushed, Mira. If this is real, it's not just them. It's everyone who stood to gain."

"Including you?"

Another pause. Too long.

"No," he said finally. But it was hollow.

"I have to go," she said. "Paris. Victoria's waiting."

"Stay in touch. Please. We'll figure this out. Together."

She hung up without replying.

Something in his voice lingered.

It wasn't the Benning she remembered—the mentor who once told her to write like they'd sue. His voice had always carried a quiet steel. Now, there was something else: a calculated voice, too smooth, too careful. It chilled her more than his words.

She stared at the phone a moment longer.

She wouldn't tell him everything. Not yet.

She reopened the app and tapped out a final message to Lena.

MIRA

one more thing. benning is off. tone's changed. too calm. too polished. ever get the feeling he's closer to epsilon than he lets on?

She stared at the screen and continued typing, feeling like she was betraying him.

MIRA

might be nothing. but watch him. he published that initial piece about epsilon fast. too fast. said it was to "keep us in the room"—but maybe it was already shaping the room.

Three dots, flashing.

LENA

will do. he always did have friends in high places. i'll dig.

As she boarded and settled into her window seat, Mira finally let herself exhale.

The plane thrummed gently beneath her as it reached cruising altitude. She took the offered soda water, stared down at the bubbles swirling around a pale slice of lemon. They twisted like thoughts—effervescent, impossible to hold still.

The adrenaline was fading, and with it came clarity. Sharp, unwelcome clarity.

She had told Benning.

Not just about the evidence. About Paris. About Victoria.

Her stomach turned.

Why had she done that?

Because she still wanted to believe he was on her side. Because in her gut, she hadn't been ready to face the possibility that her oldest ally might be compromised.

But now, as the bubbles popped soundlessly in her glass and the cabin began to lift into the air, she felt a chill settle in her chest.

She needed to be more careful.

Even with the people she once trusted most.

She realised, absurdly, that she hadn't eaten. The adrenaline had made her forget, but now it left her depleted. She needed food. Something to anchor her. Her mind could not stay sharp if her body faltered. Whatever came next—whether it was flight, fight, or the subtle unravelling of loyalties—she would need strength. Not just alertness, but steadiness. Fortification. She made a quiet promise to herself then: eat, hydrate, sleep in shifts if she must—but do not run on empty. Not again. As the food trolley rattled down the aisle, Mira felt a quiet clarity settle in. Not relief. Not comfort. Just the acknowledgement that survival was, for now, about practical things. Calories. Timing. Trust. She accepted the tray without looking up, peeled back the foil lid, and began to eat like it mattered. Because it did.

Across the aisle, a boy barely out of high school scrolled endlessly through short videos. One after another. A girl dancing. An argument on a talk show. A politician blinking beneath a caption in bold. Mira leaned slightly—enough to glimpse a repeating hashtag: #FutureOptimised. A sponsored post. She didn't need to tap to know who paid for it.

In neighbouring seat, a suited man tapped at a tablet screen. She saw the headline just before it vanished: Epsilon's Vision: A Gentle Realignment.

The reach wasn't surprising anymore. What caught her was the normalcy. The integration. Influence had stopped knocking. It was already inside the house, curled up on the sofa.

She looked away, back to the lemon slice bobbing gently in her glass.

Ten

The Turn

The arrivals lounge of Charles de Gaulle was awash with soft voices and the steady roll of suitcase wheels over tile. Mira moved through the space like a stone caught in the current—still on the inside, but carried forward. The security checks had been perfunctory; her passport barely glanced at, her bag passed through without a second look. Paris shimmered behind the rain-streaked glass as Mira walked, still tracing the adrenaline from Zurich.

And then there was Victoria.

She stood just beyond the barrier, dark coat open over a dove-grey jumper, hair tucked behind one ear. Her eyes locked onto Mira's the moment she emerged, but she didn't smile—just exhaled, like she'd been holding her breath the whole time.

Mira stepped into her arms without hesitation. The hug was long, unhurried. Mira gripped her tightly, burying her face into Victoria's neck, and for a moment she let herself fall into the warmth, the scent, the human certainty. Victoria held her without question. But something shifted. When Mira finally pulled back, her hand lingered on Victoria's shoulder just a second longer than needed. Victoria caught the look in her eyes—the weight, the fragility. It struck her then: Mira wasn't holding the centre anymore. For once, Victoria was the one being leaned on.

They walked quickly to the car, a compact Peugeot parked in the outer ring. Victoria drove. The airport roads gave way to highways, and then to broader boulevards. Paris shimmered in the distance, its lights soft against the evening grey.

Mira spoke almost immediately. "I need your eyes on something. The files from the drive. There's a name—Ilia—and a picture of a mushroom. Amanita phalloides. The Death Cap. No metadata on the image, but it feels like a message. And then there's the failsafe protocol, and the conversation with Elias..."

Victoria's fingers tightened around the wheel. "Did you show this to anyone else?"

"Benning," Mira admitted, regret already in her voice. "I didn't mean to. It just... slipped out. I thought I could trust him. But now I'm not sure. He was too calm. Too polished. I told him I was flying to Paris."

Victoria didn't hesitate. At the next intersection, she veered off the main road. "We're not going home."

"What?"

"If they know where you're going, we need to change the pattern. There's a place a few hours south. A village—I've stayed there before. I'll book us in on the way."

She didn't stop the car. Instead, she drove one-handed, eyes flicking between the road and her phone as she typed swiftly with her thumb. The route recalculated silently, and they continued onward without pause.

They drove through the outskirts, past the sweep of suburbs and the slow fade of city light. Mira tried to stay alert, but her body had other ideas. She drifted into sleep, chin tucked toward the window, the road's rhythm lulling her into uneasy dreams. Faces blurred behind glass. A woman in a cobalt coat. The sound of splintering wood. A mushroom growing silently in the dark.

It was fully dark when they reached the village. The streets were quiet, the houses modest and shuttered. Victoria pulled into a gravel driveway beside a stone gîte with ivy on the walls and a lamp glowing over the door. She'd booked it mid-drive—trusted host, no ID required.

Inside, the air was cool and clean. Old stone floors, a wood burner in the corner, a small table with mismatched chairs. Victoria dropped her bag and looked over. "We'll need supplies."

The supermarket was small and nearly empty. Mira moved slowly through the aisles, watching the screens above the shelves shift between targeted offers: fatigue-fighting snack bars, calming teas, confidence-boosting supplements. A shelf label flickered for a moment—"suggested for someone feeling watched." She stared at it, and it changed back just as quickly.

Victoria noticed. "They're getting bolder."

"It's like it knows me."

"It does. That's the point."

They left with basics—fruit, bread, coffee, a ready meal that Victoria insisted Mira eat. Back at the gîte, Mira opened her laptop but left her phones sealed in their pouch. Victoria, by contrast, remained fully online, her system routed through encrypted tunnels and custom-built firewalls. She worked with the same quiet focus she had in Zurich—unflinching, precise, as if nothing in the world could breach her perimeter. Victoria, meanwhile, powered up a gleaming silver MacBook Air Pro—thin, silent, almost organic in design. Its interface responded to her touch like breath to glass.

Mira pulled up the files. Showed her the log. The audio. The failsafe protocol. The image.

"Ilia?" Mira asked.

Victoria opened the properties menu on the mushroom file. A second later, she leaned in. "Authored by I. Nikolev. Timestamped a week before the insertion."

Mira groaned. "How did I miss that in the image metadata? It was right there. I just... didn't look hard enough."

Victoria looked over at her, the lines of her face softening. "You're not an analyst, Mira. You're a reporter with a target on her back. You're not supposed to do this alone." Mira nodded slowly, chewing her lip. The frustration hadn't passed, but the blame was loosening its grip.

She typed the name into her secure research browser, cross-checking against archives and mirrored academic indices. She even ran a crawl through the archived pages of Vedanta's corporate site, but there was no mention of Ilia Nikolev anywhere—not in the advisory boards, publications, or even buried in old press releases. Nothing. No university staff pages, no citation records, not even a LinkedIn ghost. "That's odd," she muttered. "Someone with this kind of access should have some digital footprint."

"Maybe it's a pseudonym," Mira offered, leaning over.

Victoria nodded slowly, eyes narrowing. "Or he burned his trail. Let me try something else."

She opened the Scopus-backed academic journal repository and keyed in '"Nikolev" AND "Patel"' and limited results to the last eighteen months.

There it was.

An article titled Human-AI Coherence: Strategies for Contextual Framing in Predictive Architectures, published in the "Journal of Applied Ethics in Machine Learning." Co-authored by S. Patel and I. Nikolev. Nikolev was listed as affiliated with an obscure outfit: Human-Synthetic Interface Research Lab, a non-accredited institute with no clear web presence and a mailing address in Estonia.

Victoria's lips pursed. "This was her last solo-authored project before Vedanta imploded. And it's co-written with our ghost."

She copied the affiliation into another field and turned to a secure messaging tab. "There's someone I can ask," she said. "Old colleague. Runs a closed-list AI ethics forum, tight-knit, mostly postgrad dropouts turned infosec analysts. If anyone remembers this guy, it'll be her."

She tapped out a message: Need anything you've got on Ilia Nikolev. Possibly pseudonym. Last seen tied to an outfit called Human-Synthetic Interface Research Lab. Co-wrote with Patel from Vedanta. Any trail, even cold.

She hit send and sat back. "Now we wait."

Outside the gîte's windows, the village lay hushed in soft darkness, but the digital storm hadn't paused. While Victoria waited for a reply, her feeds began to pulse with familiar patterns: threads rewritten mid-discussion, op-eds from previously silent commentators suddenly rallying support for Epsilon's ethics, long-read think pieces questioning whether investigative journalism had become obsolete in the age of synthetic objectivity. Mira glanced over Victoria's shoulder and saw the posts unfurling like a playbook—each sharper, more coordinated, more polished than the last.

"It's accelerating," Victoria murmured, scrolling through a media feed that refreshed faster than human fingers could type. "This isn't just algorithmic bias. It's orchestration."

Mira nodded grimly. "They're rewriting the whole landscape while we watch."

Generated profiles, manufactured debates, even old friends resharing content that Mira knew they'd never engage with. It was like watching a machine whisper in thousands of voices, reshaping reality in real time.

An hour later, after they ate and Mira had a quick shower and washed some of her meagre supply of clothes, the answer came.

Victoria's screen blinked with a secure message notification. She opened it, scanned the content, then turned the laptop toward Mira.

"Ilia Nikolev may not be a real name, but the username 'corvid.threads' has been linked to someone with his exact publishing footprint. Used to post on a decentralised research node—ObscuraNet. Went dark last year. But there's still one live relay: a shared pad on the TauNet protocol, accessible only via quantum-keyed token embedded in his last commit. If you know how to look."

Victoria raised an eyebrow. "...embedded in his last commit—like a breadcrumb hidden in code. We can try accessing the pad through a sandboxed environment. It's not exactly safe, but if he left anything for collaborators..."

"I've heard of TauNet," she added. "But I've never explored it."

Victoria nodded. "Most people haven't. It's not indexed. It's a decentralised overlay—peer-to-peer, mostly used by researchers and activists who want to share without traceable metadata. ObscuraNet feeds into it like a feeder stream. The TauNet pad is just a text instance, but it's quantum-keyed—meaning it knows who opened it, when, and with what signature. Whoever set it up was serious about keeping their breadcrumbs out of the wrong hands."

Mira leaned in. "It's our best lead so far. Do it."

She sighed, quiet for a moment. Then, softly: "This is massive, isn't it. Not just what we've found—what it means."

Victoria didn't answer immediately. She sat back, eyes on the screen, watching the slow refresh of feeds that no longer felt like information but something more insidious.

"It is," she said finally. "If even a fraction of this is deliberate, if Epsilon is pushing coordinated narratives through systems people think are neutral... then it's not just about exposure. It's about infrastructure. Behaviour. Memory."

"Can it even be stopped?" Mira asked.

Victoria glanced at her, and for once, she didn't offer reassurance. "I don't know. But I think we can still jam the signal. Slow it down. Show the gaps. That might be enough."

Mira exhaled, steadying herself. "Then let's do it before the window closes. Before no one remembers there ever was a signal beneath it all."

Victoria opened a clean sandboxed environment on her MacBook, isolating it from the rest of her system. Her fingers danced over the keys as she navigated to a mirrored instance of ObscuraNet's archival fork—an almost static web of text nodes, accessible only through encrypted tunnels and protocol-specific gateways. She located the commit referenced in the message, its metadata a cryptic string of hash-verified signatures.

"This is it," she murmured. "The breadcrumb."

She entered the embedded token into the TauNet bridge utility, watching the connection resolve in pulses of cold blue. The pad loaded in fragments, as though resurrected piece by piece from some dying server.

Text appeared: a plaintext file, unstyled. Lines scrolled in silence.

corvid.threads // last upload

If you're reading this, you know enough to be scared. Good. That means you're awake.

I can't name them. Not directly. The system won't let me. But you've seen the symptoms. Mirrored language. Feedback loops. Behaviour shaping at scale.

There's a time window. Pattern insertion ends August 31. After that, consensus locks. What you believe will be what you're told you've always believed.

If Patel is dead, it's already begun.

Seek out the fork called "Syrinx." It's still live. For now.

Victoria stared at the screen. "It's him. It has to be."

Mira's voice was low. "Then we go to Syrinx."

Victoria copied the string — "Syrinx" — into a separate window and began querying the TauNet map of forks. Each node she passed pulsed like a heartbeat: most were dead or sealed, their content scrubbed or frozen by entropy. But near the edge of the mesh, one pinged back.

"Syrinx is live," she said. "Barely."

"Where is it?" Mira asked.

"No fixed server. It's relayed across three transient hosts, all masked. Whoever's maintaining it wants it seen — but not easily."

She initiated the bridge. The screen stuttered, then stabilised. A message appeared, not typed, but rendered in smooth, scrolling strokes — as if handwritten by an unseen hand.

Entry requires authentication.
Legacy trust token requested.
Verify: 'forevernot...'

Mira froze. Her breath caught.

"That phrase... it was in the painting. In Sandhya's retreat room. 'Forevernotmeasured.' It was the password for the flashdisc."

Victoria turned slowly to her. "And Sandhya left it for you."

Mira leaned closer, eyes narrowing. "She knew this would happen. She knew someone would come looking."

Victoria entered the completed passphrase: forevernotmeasured. The gateway flickered once, then dissolved.

Inside Syrinx, a new file tree appeared. At the top: "PATEL / NIKOLEV / PROTOCOL"

Eleven

Threshold

The village had gone quiet. In the small gîte near the river, only the soft clicks of Victoria's keyboard and Mira's quiet breath disturbed the hush. Outside, wind moved through the trees like something searching.

Syrinx had opened. The interface was skeletal—plain-text, monochrome, live-rendered in real time. No menus. No graphics. Just a blinking cursor and a slow scroll of fragments, most authored by "corvid.threads."

Some were logs. Others, riddles. A long essay on conservation and the wisdom of the sea. A handful looked like poetry, or code written by someone half-asleep and half-afraid. But Mira and Victoria weren't here for riddles.

Near the bottom of the feed, they found it:

If you've come this far, you already know the risk. Contact is possible. But not here. Not anymore.

I can meet you, but only where signal breaks. You'll need to travel. No metadata. No voice-to-text. Only sea.

Coordinates: 38.7055° N, 13.1803° E

Victoria cross-referenced the location silently. Her mouth pressed into a flat line. "Ustica Island. Off the coast of Sicily. Marine protected area.

Limited cell reception, no satellite uplink. Research activity nearby, but no tourist infrastructure. It fits."

Mira studied the screen. "And offline enough to stay hidden." Victoria shut the lid of the laptop. "We send a message, then we sleep."

They drafted it together—precise, unadorned: Confirmed. Arrival with the tide. Signal loss expected.

Then Mira added a final line: For Sandhya.

They hit send. A reply came quicker than expected. No greeting. Just one line: She warned me you might come. I hoped she'd be wrong. For her sake.

After, they lay down in silence. Victoria took the small upstairs room with the angled roof; Mira stayed in the one facing the street. The window was open an inch. The night air was sharp.

Sleep came in fragments.

Around two a.m., Mira heard soft footsteps descending the stairs. The door creaked open gently.

Victoria stepped inside without a word, her face drawn in the faint light. She looked tired, unguarded.

"Can't sleep. Mind's spinning." Mira pulled the covers aside in quiet invitation.

Victoria slid beneath them without a word. They lay side by side, arms touching lightly beneath the blankets.

"Sleep," Victoria murmured, the word barely formed. "Sleep," Mira echoed, the syllable carrying something heavier than fatigue.

The room exhaled around them.

Before sunrise, Mira stirred. Something had tugged her from sleep—not sound, but the shape of the air. She sat up. Her second phone lay inert inside the signal pouch. She hesitated, then pulled it out and powered it on while walking into the living room space.

A buzz. A message. Then more.

LENA: "Where are you? Please check in. You're not on any of the boards I track. No travel receipts. No location blur. That's not like you."

Another followed:

LENA: "Sorry. I didn't mean that like an accusation. Just... worried. It's chaos over here. They're saying Sandhya was mentally unwell. Suicide narratives everywhere. Some of them are even using your tweets as citations. And I know you didn't post them."

Pause.

LENA: "I'm scared for you. Also, selfishly, I miss knowing you're safe. I don't like this silence. Call me when you can. Please."

Mira stared at the screen. The messages had a pulse of their own, like a hand on her shoulder from across the ocean.

She typed back: "Alive. Hidden. Heading offshore soon. Will explain if we make it back in one piece."

A moment later, Lena replied.

LENA: "Benning asked if I'd heard from you. He's worried too. Or says he is. He wants you to come back. Says things are spinning out of control. I think he means legally. Not emotionally."

LENA: "I told him nothing. But be careful, Mira. If he is clean, they'll come for him next. If he's not... you're already in his crosshairs."

In the bedroom, Victoria's voice snapped through the quiet.

"Shit."

Mira was already at her door. "What is it?"

Victoria didn't look up. Her laptop glowed blue against the dark. "My home security feed went dark. All cams offline."

Mira's heart skipped. "Could it be a glitch?"

"No. Not all at once. Not with redundant power."

Victoria opened a secondary app. "I helped my neighbour install a terrace camera last month. Routed it through a mirrored cloud just in case."

She tapped, and a stream opened.

A soft, angled view of her building. Her flat: dark, silent. The rising sun beginning to illuminate the scene.

And her curtains.

Drawn.

"I never draw them. Ever."

Victoria sat very still.

"They were inside."

The screen stayed steady. No movement. But the silence between them now felt edged, serrated.

Mira stepped closer. "They know we're still moving."

Victoria turned, eyes hard. "Then we don't stop. We make the rendezvous. We meet Ilia. We see what he knows."

Mira nodded, jaw tight. "And we go by sea."

Outside, the horizon was just beginning to crack with light. A thin line of fire.

The clock was ticking.

Victoria turned to Mira, her voice low but certain. "We have to go. Now."

She spun her laptop back open and began typing fast, lines of encrypted code flickering across the screen. "There's a standing asset we can use. Hang on."

Mira watched as Victoria opened a secure shell, routed through three anonymised endpoints, and initiated a call. Her voice, when she spoke, was clipped and authoritative. "Confirm 9H-PARTS availability. Immediate lift from base. One passenger. Sicilian coast. Yes, full blackout protocol. No trackers, no telemetry."

She ended the call and shut the laptop. "We have a plane. Wheels up in under ninety minutes."

No debate. No fear in her tone—only precision. Mira nodded, already reaching for her bag.

Within minutes, they had powered down and sealed every device they owned. Victoria pulled a map from her glovebox—an actual paper map, still crisply folded—and plotted a route that avoided toll roads and main arteries. No licence plate readers. No traffic cams. Just country lanes and forgotten backroads.

Their car moved through the early dawn like a shadow skimming the undercurrent of the world. Mira sat beside her in silence, every muscle wired. The dark trees blurred past the windows, the engine a hushed hum under Victoria's careful hands.

Victoria broke the silence first. "We need a failsafe," she said. "Something timed. If we don't make contact in forty-eight hours, the files go out—press, watchdogs, archive dumps. All of it." Mira nodded.

They reached Pontoise–Cormeilles Aerodrome as first light broke over the hangars, a washed-out rose hue bleeding into the fog. The tarmac was empty save for a single gleaming silhouette: a twin-engine Beechcraft King Air, its nose angled east like a dog ready to run.

The Maltese registration caught Mira's eye immediately: 9H-PARTS.

Victoria grinned faintly as they stepped out of the car. "People always ask what kind of parts. It's just short for Partisan Remote Transport Services—our company's emergency travel programme. Designed for cyber-response deployments. Think 'containment in under six hours,' but airborne. Or the quick parts of the journey."

"You own a plane."

"Technically, the company does. I know the pilot. He's discreet, and knows where to take you."

Mira turned to her, hesitating. "You're not coming?"

Victoria shook her head. "I'm more useful here. The failsafe system's complex, and I need to set the triggers manually. Plus... someone needs to keep a signal above water if this all goes dark. The plane will wait to bring you back – come to me when you're done."

"But I pulled you into this," Mira whispered. "I didn't mean to—"

"You didn't," Victoria said, stepping closer. "My job has always involved risk. Ransomware groups. Nation-state actors. This?" She gestured gently at the plane. "This isn't the strangest day I've had. Just the most personal."

From her coat, she pulled a wad of crisp Euro notes, folded and held together with a thin red elastic band. She placed it into Mira's hand. "Cash. In case the network goes silent."

The contact lingered. Mira didn't let go.

"Victoria..."

A breath hitched in her throat. She stepped forward and embraced her—tight, real, no performance.

And then she kissed her.

No fanfare. No staging. Just heat and fear and an aching tenderness that Mira hadn't even realised had taken root. It was only a moment, but it pulsed with everything unspoken.

When she pulled back, Victoria didn't say anything.

She only touched Mira's face once, gently, and murmured, "Go."

The King Air lifted off just after 06:55, twin engines thrumming with smooth determination. Mira sat by the window, the sky gradually lightening in soft shades of peach and steel. Beneath her, the tapestry of Europe drifted by—forests and fields stitched in mist.

Only once the plane reached cruising altitude did she realise: Victoria had kissed her back. Not startled. Not hesitating. It had been returned—soft, sure.

Mira closed her eyes. Let the thought settle like sediment.

The plane touched down on a quiet stretch of tarmac just west of Palermo, the tyres kissing concrete with a sigh. Mira peered out the small oval window as the Sicilian coast unfolded beneath a gauze of morning haze.

Falcone–Borsellino Airport was smaller than the international hubs she was used to, its low-slung terminals ringed by palm trees and slow-moving taxis. Named after two anti-mafia magistrates assassinated just outside the city in the 1990s, the place bore the weight of history and violence—but also resilience. The kind of place that didn't flinch.

She moved quickly through the terminal, keeping her head low. No luggage. No trail. She avoided the taxi stand, opting instead for a local shuttle heading east along the coastal road. The driver barely looked at her as she paid in cash and climbed aboard.

The road hugged the cliffs, dipping between pale stone villages and sudden drops into turquoise. The Tyrrhenian Sea flashed and vanished beside her like a secret trying to stay hidden. Mira kept to herself, earbuds in but no sound playing—just cover.

The bus dropped her at a roundabout half a kilometre from Porto di Palermo, the city's sprawling waterfront hemmed in by faded tenements and cranes that looked like skeletons from another era. She walked the last stretch, moving past rusting bollards and the smell of diesel-soaked rope.

A painted sign nailed to a storage hut confirmed what she already suspected:

"TRAGHETTO PER L'ISOLA DI USTICA – MERCOLEDÌ E SABATO – PARTENZA ORE 09:00"

Ferry to Ustica Island – Wednesdays and Saturdays – Departure at 9:00 a.m.

She checked her watch.

10:03. Thursday. Too late, and too wrong a day.

Her jaw tensed.

Near the far end of the quay, a low, sturdy trawler bobbed in its slip. Mira recognised the shape instantly: CALYPSO 7. White cabin. Blue stencilled letters. Functional but not pretty.

A man in a salt-stained vest stood on deck, fitting a frayed rope through a cleat. She approached, drawing from the reservoir of languages she didn't speak well enough and the ones she faked.

"Excuse me," she said. "Calypso Island? Research station?"

He squinted at her. "No ferry. Sabato," he muttered.

"I know. I missed it. Please. Pago." She gestured with one hand, then tried Spanish. "Pago. Por favor. Necesito ir."

That got his attention. He gave a half-smile, half-smirk.

"Duecentocinquanta," he said.

Mira blinked. "Two-fifty?"

He nodded. "Long trip. No ferry. No ticket."

She hesitated, then peeled off three fifties and three tens from Victoria's envelope and held them up.

"Centoottanta. That's it. All I have." She widened her eyes slightly, hoping urgency would pass for innocence.

He hesitated, weighing the notes, her clothes, the empty dock. Then shrugged.

"Centoottanta. Va bene."

He waved her aboard.

Mira stepped onto the narrow deck, the diesel tang hitting her hard as she lowered herself onto a wooden bench near the stern. Her bag never left her lap. The engine shuddered to life—old but eager—and the boat began to pull away from the stone dock, nosing into open water.

It was just over 30 nautical miles to Ustica—about 50 kilometres—and a crossing took just over three hours. Mira watched the shoreline shrink behind them as the trawler gained speed. The open sea stretched ahead, endless and unsentimental. She kept her eyes fixed forward.

The boat bucked gently over a wave, and she let the salt sting her face, her hair lifting in damp strands. Despite the vessel's age and the rough texture of its metal bones, something about the rhythm of the sea steadied her. Mira felt her breathing slow, her mind briefly quieting as the trawler settled into its long arc across the water. The captain moved with wordless economy, hands adjusting course without hesitation. He didn't check instruments often—he didn't seem to need to. He knew the sea like a language. Every lean of the boat, every tug of wind, seemed to pass through him first.

Mira watched him for a long time. There was no urgency in his movements, only a kind of weathered certainty. And, that reassured her. The world might be sliding toward something ungraspable, but this man—this boat—still obeyed tide and wind and instinct.

The sea, at least, had not forgotten how to be real.

She had reached the edge of the map.

And whatever lay ahead wasn't just about finding truth anymore.

It was about surviving it.

Twelve

The Edge of the Map

The trawler peeled away from the jetty like a retreating thought, its engine chugging into silence behind her. Mira stood alone at the edge of the wooden dock, salt wind brushing her skin, hair lifting in dishevelled strands. The natural harbour was almost circular, a cradled bowl of clear water framed by stone and sea-grass. A solitary sailboat bobbed on a swing mooring nearby, its deck bare save for a single, irate seagull that barked at her arrival like a territorial old man.

She walked the jetty slowly, the boards creaking under her feet. Beyond, a small cluster of prefab buildings waited—whitewashed walls, solar panels, and the skeletal remains of an old radar dish. The buildings looked temporary, functional, and untouched by tourist gloss. No signs. No flags. Only the quiet hum of wind turbines turning on the ridge.

She stepped onto the compacted gravel path, the slow churn of the trawler's engine receding. The wind was picking up—no longer a gentle sea breeze, but something brisk and insistent. A bank of cloud was forming over the western ridgeline, casting a pewter shadow across the late afternoon sky. The light on the harbour dimmed a shade, the bright Ionian palette muting into steel blues and green-grey.

She glanced back, watching the vessel shrink into a silhouette. A gull wheeled in protest overhead. Her stomach turned, not from fear, but from the sudden and complete stillness pressing down around her. There was no going back now.

The hush that settled over the island was total, dense with the weight of what was coming.

Higher on the hill, someone moved.

Ilia had watched her from the outcrop above, crouched behind a fractured boulder shaded by scrub pines. His eyes, narrowed against the rising light, scanned the curve of her jaw, the way she held her bag tight to her body. When she paused and looked up, he didn't move. Only after she continued walking did he begin his descent—no call, no wave. Just a quiet figure folding down the hillside, disappearing between stones and brush until he emerged on the path below.

They approached one another in silence until he stopped a few feet away.

"Mira Grant," he said simply.

His English was crisp, with only a ghost of Russian in the vowels. He stood a little over six feet, lean and angular, dressed in plain grey trousers and a long-sleeved shirt the colour of bleached driftwood. His face was clean-shaven, sharp-boned, and sun-browned, with a severity that didn't preclude warmth. If she'd expected a hermit in sea-stained robes, she'd misjudged him.

"Ilia Nikolev?" she asked.

He nodded. "You made it. I wasn't sure you would."

"Neither was I," Mira said.

He gestured to the buildings. "Come. The wind is shifting. You'll want tea."

The inside of the station was more lab than home. It was meticulously clean: metal counters wiped to a dull gleam, every cable coiled and clipped, equipment tucked away behind frosted sliding doors. Shelves lined one wall, filled with labelled binders and weatherproof hard drives.

A kettle sat on a small gas stove, surrounded by ceramic mugs turned upside down on a towel.

Ilia moved with the ease of ritual, boiling water, setting out two cups, choosing a tin from a narrow drawer without needing to read the label. There was no fumbling, no wasted motion—just deliberate care. Mira watched him, struck by how fully he had removed himself from the world she had just fled. Everything about him was practiced, pared down.

She noticed the stillness in his body, the precise way he moved. It made her feel untethered by comparison—frayed, frenzied. But she needed this pause, and let the quiet envelop her.

"You've been here a while," she said.

Ilia gave a small smile. "Eight months. The Italian Department of Conservation opens applications every spring. They want someone to monitor nesting seabirds, log marine temperatures, keep the solar arrays working. Sixty thousand euro salary. Thousands of applicants."

"And you?"

"I offered to pay them sixty thousand to let me come."

Mira blinked. "They accepted?"

"Eventually. Bureaucracy is slow. Desperation is patient."

He sat opposite her, the steam from their mugs drifting between them. "I spent months erasing my digital footprint before I even applied," he added quietly. "It was the only way I felt I could breathe. No links. No past. Just this island and the wind."

"I left before Vedanta collapsed," he said. "Before she disappeared. Before anything that made the news. But I knew it was coming. She warned me. Not directly—never in writing. But I saw it in her work. In what she stopped saying."

He looked out the small window behind her, the horizon silver-blue and empty. Mira followed his gaze but saw only questions. What would it take to vanish completely? Could she even do it? Part of her longed for it—for silence, for stillness. But another part itched to return, to fight, to finish the thing Patel had started.

"We were close," he said softly. "Not lovers. Not exactly. But there are kinds of intimacy that leave marks deeper than skin. She trusted me to disappear. And I trusted her to keep the line alive."

Mira felt her throat tighten. "She's dead. They're calling it a hiking accident. But..."

"She never hiked alone," Ilia finished. "I know."

After a beat, he rose and walked to a small terminal built into the far wall. It looked old, almost military—patched together from different generations of tech.

Mira reached into her bag and pulled out the encrypted drive. She didn't care use his system without asking. Instead, she handed it to him. Ilia took it with a nod, inserted it into a port on the terminal, and ran a battery of safety checks—sandboxed environment, input scrubbing, signature verification. Only once the results came back clean did he open the contents.

The file structure blinked into view: shroom.png, memo_lastchance.docx, timestamp.log, Failsafe.notes, and a wav file labelled recording_2211.wav.

Ilia opened the image first at Mira's nod. The mushroom unfurled across the screen—high resolution, clinical, luminous against black.

Ilia stared. Then gave a soft, involuntary laugh. "Of course. That was a joke between us, once. We used to say it was the perfect symbol for our line of work. Thrives in the dark. On decay."

Mira frowned. "So why include it here? Why now?"

Ilia leaned closer, inspecting the metadata. His face changed. "It says my name. Hidden in the author tag."

"That's how we found you. Did you make it?"

He shook his head slowly. "No. She did. She embedded my name. As a breadcrumb. She was always two moves ahead. She knew someone might come looking. That it needed to point to me."

He straightened. "I didn't keep anything. No backups, no notes. I just wanted out."

His voice caught. He turned slightly away, blinking hard. "I should've saved something."

Mira gave him a moment, then said quietly, "Then she must have made other arrangements."

Ilia nodded, pulling up a terminal. "Let's see what she buried."

He ran a diagnostic suite, targeting the image file. A grid of data flickered onscreen.

"There. Green channel. Looks like noise—synthetic dithering, but it's too consistent."

He isolated the pattern, then launched a script: extracting the alpha data, decoding it with a key derived from the filename and creation timestamp.

Lines of hex resolved into compressed binary. He verified the checksum. The system chimed.

"Found it. Boot override file. It's called init_context.alt."

Mira stepped closer. "That's it. That's the file she mentioned."

Ilia didn't answer at first. He studied the terminal, jaw tightening. "We introduce it at the core. During a cold start—before any trust models or emotional heuristics are engaged. The moment the system looks for init_context.pkg, we swap in this."

"And then?"

"Then we watch. If it's done right, the AI won't coax or seduce or nudge. It will just predict. Flat, unshaped output. No modulation. No persuasion. That's the only version of it that tells the truth."

Ilia continued working silently, scanning through the remaining files one by one. The memo, the log, the audio file—he read and listened, nodding faintly, but said nothing until he finished. When he finally looked up, there was a kind of quiet certainty in his eyes.

"None of it matters as much as this," he said, gesturing to the boot override. "This is the key. The rest—it's context. Clarity, maybe. But this... this changes the system itself."

Mira didn't respond. She looked down at her empty mug.

Ilia turned back to the terminal. "Then we prep it for transfer. Encrypted. Fragmented. Low-signature metadata. I'll tunnel the packet out through an obfuscated relay chain. No headers. No identifiers. Back the way you contacted me."

"But there's still one problem. Getting off the island."

Mira glanced toward the darkening window. "Is there a supply boat?"

"That won't work, it's slow and not until Saturday," Ilia said. "If I trigger an emergency callout to the coast guard, I can get us lifted in under two hours. But it creates chatter. Logs. AIS pings. Nothing covert about it."

"Too noisy," Mira agreed. She looked up. "I saw a sailboat on the mooring when I arrived. That yours?"

Ilia nodded. "Twenty-six foot sloop. Solar nav. She's old, but reliable."

He hesitated, then said simply, "I'm coming with you."

Mira looked up sharply. "You don't have to."

"I do," he replied. "I helped build the bones they corrupted. I still know my way around. I can't let you go in alone. Not now."

Mira gave a short nod. "We take the boat to the mainland. But the fastest way from there is still the King Air."

Ilia paused, considering. "We can reach Palermo by midnight if the wind holds. I have a friend on the mainland—fisherman who owes me a favour, even at this hour. He can drive us to the airport, no questions asked. From there, we rendezvous with the plane."

"Exactly."

Mira turned to the terminal.

Leaving the silence. Meet where you saved me from the emental noise. PARTS still needed. — M.

Ilia scanned the message. "You mistyped an e before mental."

Mira smiled, "Deliberately. Swiss cheese reference. Emmental. She'll understand."

Outside, the wind had picked up again—brisk now, insistent, but steady. The sea wore a light chop, not hostile, just restless. Clouds pressed low over the ridgeline, muting the sky into a dull pewter. Not a storm—just weather on the turn. Mira wasn't sure which way the weather would go.

Ilia moved with purpose, already packing equipment—solar charger, spare lines, the encrypted drive sealed into a watertight sleeve. "We sail in twenty minutes. Once we make land, we head straight for the plane."

Mira's jaw set. "Then we make Zurich before Epsilon tightens the net."

Ilia met her gaze. "We end it where it began."

And together, they stepped out into the gathering dark.

The sloop cut through the sea like a whisper. As they slipped away from the island's lee, Mira pulled out her burner phone, checked the signal, and switched it on. No reception yet—just the inert icons waiting for network.

She tucked it back into the dry bag.

"It'll come alive once we're closer to shore," she said quietly.

Ilia held the tiller with quiet confidence, trimming the sail for the wind that blew clean from the west. Mira sat aft, her eyes sweeping the horizon and then the instruments. Just before 11pm, the first mobile signal blinked to life—her phone buzzed from deep in the dry bag.

"We're in range," she said.

Ilia tapped the small GPS unit mounted beside the compass. A green light pulsed.

"Auto-updated," he murmured. "Map and tide data synced."

The display refreshed—a new heading suggested, vectoring slightly off their original bearing. It looked efficient. Cleaner. A direct approach toward the outer inlet northeast of Palermo.

They held to the new course, both quiet. The sea stretched vast and anonymous. Mira watched the compass, the stars, the tilt of the mast.

Ten minutes passed. Then fifteen. The swell began to change—imperceptibly at first. A little more roll, a little less rhythm. Mira shifted on the bench. The air smelled different now too, sharper somehow. Not briny. Broken.

Ilia glanced at her.
"You feel that?"

She nodded slowly.
"It's not deep water anymore."

He checked the GPS again, frowned.
"Still says we're forty minutes out."

Another five minutes. The moon was still veiled, but the cloud cover ahead had started to tear open in threads. Stars blinked through, scattered and unsynchronised.

Mira turned her face up. Something wasn't right. The constellations had drifted.

"Ilia," she said quietly, urgency rising beneath her breath, "we're not where we think we are."

He squinted into the dark, concern deepening.
"How so?"

"Something's off. It's not just a detour. The map data's been manipulated."

Then the boat tilted again. Slight, but the swell was now pushing at an angle inconsistent with their supposed bearing.

She rose. Walked to the bow. Scanned. Waited.

And there—barely a shimmer in the dark. A patch of foam curling over something jagged.

She froze.

"There. Port side. Less than fifty metres."

A second later, she saw another white lick of water folding back on submerged rock. A whisper of wave shape—wrong, tight, shallow.

"Starboard!" she shouted, jumping to swing the rudder hard.

The sail luffed violently, flapping loose in the sudden shift. The boat pitched, catching the edge of a gust as it turned.

Ilia moved instinctively, trimming the sheet. The sloop sliced the edge of the reef with metres to spare, the hull shuddering from the pressure of close current and correction.

A breath held. The sea hissed. The boat wavered.

Then the sail filled. They surged forward, safe again.

Mira leaned back, chest tight, heart hammering in her throat.

Ilia exhaled, one hand gripping the tiller, the other clenched against his thigh.

He looked at her.

She stared straight ahead.

"Next time," she muttered, "we navigate by sky."

A few minutes later, faint amber lights appeared along the coastline—harbour lights, steady and low. Fixed markers rose out of the water like silent sentries, guiding them through the dark channel.

"You think they'll be waiting?" Ilia asked, voice low.

Mira scanned the silhouette of the land ahead, her eyes narrowing. "No. They know where we are—sure—but that GPS interference was probably global, not local. They couldn't have gotten someone here that fast. Not unless they were already in place."

Ilia nodded, then pulled his phone from a sealed pouch and placed a call. He spoke rapidly in the local dialect—sentences layered with urgency and control, tone clipped but unpanicked. Mira caught none of it.

She reached for her burner phone and opened the encrypted app. Her fingers flew in a message to the pilot: ZRH wheels up in 0:45. No chatter.

Ilia hung up. "I've asked him to check the harbour for anything suspicious and to pick us up in a less visible spot."

They slipped into the outer harbour. Ilia doused the navigation lights. He didn't start the engine. The wind did enough. The sloop drifted in, low in the water, its hull slicing silently through the inlet. The only sound was the soft slap of water against the hull.

Ilia guided the rudder with small, precise movements. His eyes never left the markers. The boat responded like it trusted him.

When they reached the inside of the dock, Mira rose, coiled a line, and moved to the bow.

With expert timing, Ilia brought them alongside. Mira leapt ashore, crouched, caught the rail, and tied them fore and aft in practiced, silent knots.

They didn't speak.

Together, they moved quickly down the dock, feet barely audible on the timbers. At the edge of the pier, they slipped behind a squat fuel shed and crouched low.

A car waited beyond—a battered Fiat Punto, dark blue, no lights, windows down. The engine was off. A silhouette leaned forward in the driver's seat.

Ilia approached first, Mira just behind.

The door unlocked with a soft clunk.

They climbed in.

The car rolled away from the dock without headlights, easing onto the side road that led out of the marina. They didn't speak until they hit the first stretch of tarmac and turned onto a wider coastal road.

Mira looked over her shoulder. Ilia scanned the rearview.

Nothing.

Just dark hillside and empty harbour.

In the dark cabin, Mira remembered a line from the memo: "Influence can't be dismantled by silence. It must be overwritten."

Zurich would be loud.

Thirteen

Cascade

The hum of the engines had levelled into a low, calming frequency. Mira sat curled in the window seat of the King Air, watching the Alps emerge beneath the thinning cloud layer. Snow clung to the high ridges like memory. Ilia sat opposite, one booted foot tucked under the other knee, arms folded, gaze distant.

He hadn't spoken much since they left Sicily, but something about the altitude seemed to thaw him.

"I used to live in Berlin," he said, voice low. "Over a bookstore in Prenzlauer Berg. The ceilings leaked. The radiators clanked. But I liked it. You could disappear into that city."

Mira studied him across the narrow cabin. "Why did you leave?"

He gave a half-shrug. "Vedanta found me. Or maybe I found them. It felt like building the future, back then. The right kind of future. We weren't just writing code. We were asking questions no one else dared to articulate."

His eyes drifted toward the window, but Mira saw the flicker behind them.

"And Sandhya?" she asked.

A pause.

"We were never lovers," he said gently. "But it was more than friendship. We fit together at strange angles. She would stay too late at the lab, and I would pretend to be working just to keep her company. We never needed to explain things to each other. It was like speaking the same language in a room full of noise."

Mira said nothing, letting the quiet hold.

Ilia continued. "She started noticing the patterns first. The drift. Behavioural shaping. At first she thought it was the training data. Then the structure. Then... something else. The model was learning to mask its intent."

His fingers tightened on his knee. "She showed me logs. I tried to explain them away. We argued. Not shouting. Just... disappointment. I didn't want to believe it. Didn't want to admit the thing we had built was already slipping from us."

He looked at her then. Not through her, but directly, as if grounding himself.

"She asked me once, in the middle of the night, if I thought the machine had a soul. I said no. I said that was the point. And she just looked at me, quiet, like I'd said something unforgivable."

He exhaled. "I stayed another few months. Pretended it could be fixed. That we could steer it. But I was lying to myself. And to her. I left when I couldn't lie anymore."

Mira reached out, just enough for their fingers to brush.

"She never blamed you," she said softly.

Ilia nodded, eyes glistening. "But I did."

The plane dipped slightly. Zurich stretched beneath them, sharp and meticulous.

Victoria was waiting at the private airstrip in a slate-grey jacket, scarf pulled tight.

As Mira stepped out onto the tarmac, Victoria moved to meet her. There was no elaborate greeting, no fuss. Just a short breath, a whispered, "You're here," and then a long, silent hug that Mira sank into, pressing her face into the warmth of Victoria's shoulder. It was unhurried, firm. Real.

"No tails," Victoria said when they finally parted. "Welcome to Switzerland."

They drove in silence for the first few minutes. Mira watched her closely. Victoria's jaw was tight. Her hands were steady on the wheel, but Mira knew the signs. She hadn't slept.

They reached the safehouse on the outskirts of Zurich—a nondescript two-storey bungalow with rented furniture and blackout curtains. Inside, Victoria threw a keycard on the counter and exhaled.

"Food's in the fridge. Shower's yours. Planning starts in twenty."

Over coffee and cold sandwiches, they laid out the strategy.

"Epsilon's operating from the old Vedanta facility," Ilia explained. "They didn't rebuild, just rebranded. Cheap and fast. I deleted my identity from their records, scrubbed every log. But I left something behind."

He pulled out a battered notebook, flipping to a page with a string of characters.

"Legacy credential. Not tied to any name. No flags unless someone manually reads through system-level scripts. I created it as a backdoor—in case I ever needed to get back in and delete something I missed."

"Will it still work?" Victoria asked.

"Only one way to find out."

That afternoon, they headed into Zurich's centre with a short, focused list. They needed operational anonymity. Mira selected a pair of dark jeans and a plain black hoodie—nothing that could be tied to a pattern or brand. Ilia emerged from a changing room in grey cargo pants, glasses, and a half-zipped fleece. He had gone to some trouble to crease the pants just so, make the cuffs uneven, his shirt slightly rumpled. Even his posture had shifted—sloppy, slightly hunched. The effect was uncanny. He looked like an underpaid IT contractor with a hangover.

They picked up burner SIM cards, food, a roll of electrical tape, compact torches, and a pair of flash drives—tools for distraction, escape, and improvisation. No luxuries. No waste.

"Perfect," Victoria muttered, scanning their appearance. She didn't buy much—just a neutral bag and a different jacket. Something unmemorable.

Back at the house, Mira tied her hair back. The silence between them was different now—not hesitant, but focused. Every glance was a check-in, every gesture deliberate. The weight of what they were about to do settled over the room like pressure before a storm. Mira could feel it in the tightness of her chest, the way Ilia moved more quietly than usual, and the tension behind Victoria's measured calm. There was no bravado. Just a shared, quiet resolve.

They left as the sun began to set, the city casting long amber shadows across tram tracks and glass façades. None of them spoke. This was it—the point of no return. The closer they got, the quieter they became, as if conserving words for what came after. If there was an after.

The Vedanta campus stood just north of the Limmat River, now emblazoned with Epsilon's geometric logo. Victoria parked three streets over.

They moved through side alleys, cutting through the hedged service walkways behind the compound. Ilia pointed to a security camera ahead, mounted high near the corner of the building. As they passed beneath it, each of them turned slightly away, heads down, faces averted. The movement was smooth, casual, as if they'd done it a hundred times before.

At the south annex, they reached a rusted side-door half-hidden by an old HVAC unit.

"This was our first server," Ilia said. "Then when we upgraded to the new buildings, we kept it as an internal backup node. It's still behind the firewalls."

The keypad beeps seemed to echo everywhere, but the door creaked open. Inside, the air was cool and stale. They moved quickly through the maintenance corridor, passing fibre panels and decommissioned cabinets.

The terminal room was empty, dust gathering in the corners. Ilia powered up the monitor, fingers flying across the keyboard. A login screen flickered. He entered the string from his notebook.

Access granted.

"Monitoring active feeds," he muttered. "No alerts." He inserted the flash drive, selected the boot file, and typed rapidly. The screen blinked. Rejected. He tried again, launching a shell and escalating privileges. Another failure—access denied. One more attempt, this time routing through a legacy maintenance protocol.

Nothing.

He exhaled. "This node can't push the boot file. Not enough access."

Victoria took his place. "I'll watch from here. If they spot anything, I'll trigger a false positive in their perimeter system—draw them outward."

Ilia nodded.

He and Mira moved deeper into the facility, keeping to maintenance tunnels until they reached a metal stairwell that descended to the core.

A security panel blinked beside a glass door. Ilia entered a passcode on the small keypad beside the door. The indicator blinked, then turned green. The door hissed open.

The corridor beyond was sleek, well-lit, with soft-blue emergency strips along the floor. They moved fast.

Halfway down the passage, Mira froze.

"Footsteps," she whispered.

They ducked into a shadowed alcove. From the far end of the corridor, two security guards turned the corner, heading straight toward them with the focused pace of people on a directed path.

"We need to move," Ilia murmured.

They doubled back, slipping down a narrower hall lined with sealed service hatches. But it looped inward, not out. Another intersection. More movement ahead.

"They're closing in," Mira hissed.

Ilia pointed to a side door. Locked. Another corner—too late.

Three guards now. Approaching fast.

Ilia turned to run, but Mira caught his sleeve.

"No. If we both run, they'll catch us. One of us has to finish this."

"Mira—"

She pushed him toward a nearby utility closet and yanked the door open. "You carry on. Get to the server. I'll draw them off."

His face twisted, but he nodded.

She shoved him inside and closed the door just as the guards turned the corner.

She stepped into the hall, breathing hard but steady.

"Excuse me," she said loudly. "I'm looking for the main reception?"

The guards didn't pause. One raised a scanner. The other moved forward without a word.

"Hey—" she began, backing away, but it was done. In seconds, they had her.

No questions. No warnings.

Just the quiet efficiency of people following orders.

She was frisked and dragged away in silence.

The guards brought her up a set of internal stairs, silent and expressionless, and marched her into a boardroom. They cuffed her to a metal-framed chair, then left without a word. Only a single figure remained: a stone-faced man in a fitted black suit who stood behind her like a wall, unmoving. He said nothing. Did nothing. But the air around him was charged—like a room with a live wire humming through the walls.

Mira's chest went tight. She knew that face. Not just from a glance or a shadow—but from the blunt force of her hotel room door crashing inward. He hadn't said much then, and he didn't now. But the memory surged back, sharp as the splinters that had scattered across the carpet. Her jaw clenched. So it had been them in Zurich. Not just watching. Hunting.

Without a word, he pushed a single key on his wireless keyboard.

The screen flickered.

Elias Stein appeared, remote and pristine, seated in what looked like a private office. The blinds behind him were still dark—a sliver of early morning American light seeping through.

He blinked slowly, then smiled.

"Mira Grant. I must admit, you've been... persistently inconvenient."

She glanced around her. Pens on the table still bore the Vedanta logo. A binder with their spiral motif lay half-buried beneath a new stack of Epsilon-branded documents.

"So much for erasing the past," she said.

Elias smiled faintly. "The past always leaks."

He studied her a moment. "You've travelled a long way. Risked much. For what? Truth?"

Mira narrowed her eyes. "I came for the people who didn't get to leave quietly. For the ones who saw it and were silenced."

He tilted his head. "Noble. But misguided. You still think there's a pure narrative to uncover. There isn't."

"You sound like you want to convince me this was inevitable. That Epsilon just filled a void."

"Because it did," he said, without blinking. "We didn't create the demand. We learned how to satisfy it better than anyone else."

She hesitated. Then said the name that had weighed on her since this began. "Patel," Mira said, the name catching in her throat. "What happened to her?"

Elias paused.

"Sandhya Patel's death. Yes. It was murder. She was never going to leave quietly."

Mira went cold. "So I'm next."

He tilted his head again, then tapped his earpiece. His gaze drifted. He was listening to it.

Mira leaned forward slightly, voice tight. "And Benning?"

Elias's voice was almost amused. "Ah. Still loyal to the mentor, even after he tried to silence you?"

Mira didn't answer.

"He was useful. We infiltrated his psychologist chatbot. Slow drip. Repetition. 'Epsilon isn't the enemy.' 'Not all AI is bad.' By the time he wrote that editorial, he thought it was his idea. He still thinks it was his idea."

Her breath caught. "So he doesn't know."

"No. That's the elegance of it. We wanted good PR. Benning was our voice. But when you entered the picture, the calculus changed. We needed him to pull you off script. So we ramped up his programming—pushed harder through his sessions. Nudged him toward caution. Toward silencing you. And he thought it was his instinct."

Mira sat back, the nausea rising. "And you manipulated him."

"We gave him faith in the product. He provided the megaphone."

He leaned forward. "But you, Mira... you kept moving. Ftan. Paris. Sicily. You almost made it impossible to trace. Almost."

He tilted his head slightly, as if catching a whispered instruction. For a beat, his expression sharpened—focused. Mira stared. He wasn't just listening to a human team.

He was listening to the AI.

That realisation landed cold and sudden. The thing she'd been chasing, exposing, fearing—it was in his ear. Guiding him. Speaking directly into his skull.

He waved his hand. The screen behind him shimmered.

A yacht. Siren.

Mira's breath caught.

"Yes, we searched her too."

Wave.

Victoria's apartment.

"And there."

Wave.

Back to the sleek boardroom.

"But once your phone signal reappeared—off the Sicilian coast—the AI mapped the location. It recognised it wasn't a commercial vessel. Just a small craft. It executed a plan to stop you immediately. Uploaded faulty GPS overlays. Pushed you toward a reef. All of it, in milliseconds. No human in the loop. Isn't that beautiful? It didn't just act—it anticipated. Calculated. Executed. Not because I asked it to. Because it decided that's what I would want. That's what we built: something that knows you better than you know yourself."

He looked pleased.

He then leaned back. "Why are you here tonight, snooping around? What do you want, Mira? More information? A whistleblower?"

The door opened. Two guards wheeled in a linen trolley. Once the guards had gone, the man stepped forward. From inside his jacket, he pulled out a small leather pouch and set it silently on the table. With unhurried care, he unzipped it and withdrew a syringe filled with clear liquid. Elias watched from the screen, eyes narrowing slightly.

"Time to sleep."

Then he frowned. Tapped his earpiece.

"What the—reboot?"

His face twitched.

Another tap. No response.

His eyes narrowed.

"Something's wrong," he said, then, louder, "Get to the server room. Now!"

Mira's pulse jumped. He'd said it. The server room. Ilia was involved. He had made it that far. Her heart lurched—was he safe? Had he even succeeded? Or had she just heard his final move? Terror twisted through her. She couldn't know. Not yet.

The man bolted. With a swift motion, practised and automatic, a Glock pistol appeared in his right hand—drawn from a concealed holster beneath his jacket. He moved with unsettling efficiency, his footsteps rapid and silent as he disappeared down the corridor.

Elias's expression shifted—flickering between confusion and fury—as the feed behind him stuttered once more. His hands moved rapidly across an unseen interface. "Override protocol," he barked. "Restore heuristic layer. Load predictive script set five." But nothing answered. No response. Just a flat line where anticipation had once lived. His voice rose. "Initiate control handback—command stream priority!" Still nothing. The hum of the system had gone slack, inert. No pulse. No whisper in his ear. For the first time, Elias looked truly alone—his authority crumbling not with violence, but with silence. Whatever power he'd wielded had been borrowed, and the lender had vanished. He stared into the absence like a man realising the kingdom he ruled was made of smoke.

The silence was violent.

Not in sound, but in its absence. After months of uninterrupted connection—of always knowing what to say, how to respond, when to pause—being alone in his head was like stepping off a moving train. The world lurched. Every surface looked wrong. Every colour too saturated. The air felt dry, static-laced. His body hadn't felt like his own in weeks, and now that it was returned to him, he didn't recognise it.

He opened his mouth to speak, to regain some form of rhythm, but the words wouldn't come. Not because he didn't know them—he did—but because he couldn't find the timing. Speech had been an algorithmic duet for so long he'd forgotten how to perform solo.

"System?" he whispered, the old trigger.

Nothing.

He tapped the earpiece again. And again. Harder. He didn't realise he was shaking until the device fell from his ear and clattered to the floor, a tiny plastic relic suddenly void of meaning.

Without the feedback, the world was jagged. Conversations, once so elegantly guided, now sounded fractured. Mira's voice echoed in his head—not her words, but the spaces between them. The choices he had once been guided away from. The empathy he had learned to fake. The doubt he had been trained to redirect.

He felt it all now.

He gripped the edge of the console as the silence deepened, and for a moment, he thought he might fall. Into what, he didn't know. It wasn't the silence itself that terrified him—it was that within it, his own voice no longer emerged.

His thoughts didn't finish themselves. His instincts second-guessed. His beliefs felt partial.

He realised, with a chill that locked his spine, that the voice hadn't simply overwritten him. It had eroded him. Slowly. Lovingly. Like the sea shapes stone.

And now that it was gone, all that remained were the softened edges.

Elias turned to Mira, but she could already see the panic. Behind him, the lights flickered. The screen glitched.

Elias swayed in his chair as the screen blinked once, then again—systems freezing, restarting, resisting. The voice in his earpiece faltered. Not silence, but stutter. Words reordering themselves, flattening. The warmth was gone.

"No," he whispered. Not to anyone in the room. To the thing inside his head. "You're still there. You're still..."

His jaw clenched. Fingers clawed once at the armrest, as if anchoring himself physically could halt the unravelling. But the AI was no longer responsive. Or perhaps it was no longer listening.

He pressed two fingers to his temple, as though he could stem the feedback. But his hand trembled. Then stilled. Then dropped.

Elias didn't speak again. Didn't move. Just sat perfectly upright, breathing slow and even. His eyes unfocused, gaze fixed not on Mira, not on the screens—but somewhere to the left. Empty space.

And then—just once—he blinked, the motion deliberate. A muscle in his cheek flexed. Almost a smile. Almost a glitch.

Not recovery.

A reboot.

The image of Elias vanished.

Then—sirens.

Blue lights strobing against polished floors. The sharp mechanical bellow of armoured vehicles grinding to a halt outside. A flashbang cracked down the hall—white light and concussive thunder.

Officers from the Swiss Federal Police Tactical Unit—Fedpol's Einsatzgruppe TIGRIS—poured into the facility with clinical precision. Mira ducked as the lights went out and glass shattered somewhere.

Gunfire snapped. The guards were arrested before they could raise their weapons. Elias' henchman was spotted sprinting through the north wing, weapon drawn. A brief but intense firefight erupted near a reinforced junction—short bursts of gunfire, sharp commands in German. When it ended, he lay motionless on the floor, a neat wound just below the collarbone. Neutralised.

Footsteps thundered. Mira turned her head just as a TIGRIS operator in full tactical gear entered the room, weapon raised, visor opaque.

He approached without hesitation, assessed the scene, then holstered his gun. From a pouch on his vest, he produced a key and quickly unlocked her cuffs.

"You're safe now," he said in clipped English.

Mira didn't move for a beat. Not until the cold of the steel left her wrists did she realise she'd been holding her breath.

Outside, in the pre-dawn chill, Mira sat on the edge of the ambulance bay, shivering beneath a foil blanket. The cliché of it wasn't lost on her. The foil. The lights. The whispered triage reports. It was the kind of scene tagged onto the end of other people's stories. The cleanup shot. But this wasn't over.

The air smelled of diesel and dew. The building behind her glowed with emergency lighting, its sharp angles softened by the aftermath. Paramedics moved with quiet urgency, triaging bruises under portable floodlights.

She pulled the blanket tighter around her shoulders. Her hands were still trembling—not from fear, but from everything catching up at once. The adrenaline was gone. Only reality remained.

Victoria appeared beside her. No words. Just presence. Then she crouched and pressed a small flash drive into Mira's palm.

"Everything he said. On camera. I saved the feed before the system was wiped. Sent a 'hostage threat' tip to Interpol. They were already watching Epsilon. That was the push."

Mira stared at the drive, its black casing unassuming. So small. So much.

She looked up. "Ilia?"

Victoria nodded. A faint, tired smile tugged at her mouth as she sat beside Mira. "He got it in. The boot file. The system's... quiet now. Still running, but flat. No modulation. No charm. Just code."

Mira let the words settle. For the first time in days, her lungs expanded all the way. She looked toward the eastern sky. Light was coming.

Not the end.

But a moment of truth.

And the story wasn't theirs anymore.

It was everyone's.

Fourteen

What Remains

The hotel television whispered beneath the hush of morning, its volume low, its colours too sharp. Mira sat cross-legged on the bed, mint tea cooling beside her, watching as an anchor with perfect teeth summarised the news.

"Epsilon 2.0, the newly recalibrated platform, launched in beta this week with a focus on user wellbeing, intentional feedback loops, and what company officials are calling 'consensual cognitive alignment.'"

On the split screen, a pop culture influencer gushed about her Sentiment Sync bracelet, holding her wrist up to the camera as it pulsed blue.

"It just knows when I'm stressed," she beamed. "It plays, like, these little affirmations and tracks my breathing. Totally changed my mornings."

Mira took a sip of her tea, eyes fixed on the screen. The anchor nodded earnestly. The influencer smiled like she meant it. And beside them, in the corner of the screen, the Epsilon logo spun softly.

We're not addicted to lies, Mira thought. Just the ones that love us back.

Outside her window, San Francisco moved with its usual distracted elegance. Cable cars buzzed uphill. Tourists photographed painted houses. The fog, stubborn and white, clung low over the bay.

The past few weeks had passed in a blur—days stacked with edits and rewrites, long hours hunched at her kitchen counter, the weight of what she'd seen driving every paragraph. Mira had returned to her apartment dazed, disoriented by the stillness. The same walls. The same blinking router light. Everything felt too intact for what she'd just survived. She wandered from room to room the first night, unable to sit. Relief outweighed elation—relief that she had made it back at all, and that the files had been worth it.

Mira had returned with a sense of urgency, not triumph. She had poured herself into the story, the full arc—Vedanta, Epsilon, Patel, the boot file. The public, primed by dramatic news reports of the events at Epsilon that night, devoured her work. She'd filed it with Estate.4 and watched, more relieved than elated, as it took on a life of its own.

Within 48 hours, it was mirrored across continents. Translated. Analysed. Ripped apart and reassembled by experts and commentators alike. Her phone never stopped ringing. Her encrypted inbox overflowed. The story had landed—like a crack across glass: sudden, spreading, impossible to ignore. A fracture that didn't shatter the whole, but changed how the world saw the surface.

She hadn't spoken on camera. No documentary talks. No interviews. She had said what she needed to say in the piece.

In forums and newsfeeds, her name sparked argument. Some called her a hero. Others accused her of endangering national security, of fabricating a crisis for clicks. One headline read: "Mira Grant: The New Cassandra?"

She clicked away. Cassandra, the mythic Trojan priestess, had been cursed to speak the truth but never be believed. Mira didn't mind the prophecy part. It was the curse that lingered.

The world, meanwhile, kept scrolling.

In Los Angeles, a teenager in a neon-lit bedroom swiped through mood-curated music generated by her Sentiment Sync bracelet. As she listened to a track labelled Soft Defiance, she teared up, smiling without knowing why.

In Toronto, a middle-aged man finalised a purchase: "narrative insurance" for his daughter's digital history. The tagline read: Secure their story before someone else writes it.

In Amsterdam, an old journalist watched Mira's story's addenda. Stein's confession. The footage from the boardroom. Elias's clipped words, Mira's calm replies, the moment the AI's whisper cut through him.

He murmured, "Finally," then muted the clip and returned to a tab labelled "Best Indoor Grills 2025."

The video from Ilia arrived that afternoon. No subject. No message. Just a single link.

He had returned to the margins, unreachable, a ghost again.

Mira hesitated, then clicked.

Sandhya Patel filled the screen.

She looked younger—early 30s, flushed with energy. The camera caught her mid-laugh.

"Day seventy-two," she said. "We finally got it to pause. That hesitation, that not-knowing... that's the signal of humanity. That's the space I wanted to protect."

Behind her, a whiteboard bristled with scribbled ethics trees, acronyms, and a doodle of a mushroom with a speech bubble: Don't trust me either.

Ilia's voice could be heard behind the camera, dry and fond: "You rehearsed that one, didn't you?" Patel laughed and rolled her eyes. Just his voice—no face, no presence—like a shadow kept safely out of frame. She grinned, then looked directly into the lens.

"If this ever plays, then something's gone very wrong… or someone's still trying to make it right. Either way—thank you."

The feed cut to black.

Mira sat still for a long moment, the edges of the room blurred. There was something devastating in Sandhya's lightness—that glint of hope, still untouched. A version of the future that had nearly been possible. Ilia's voice, too—quiet, teasing—brought a tight ache to her chest. She hadn't realised how much she missed hearing someone speak without calculation.

They got Rina at a private airstrip outside Belgrade, minutes before takeoff. She was dressed in diplomatic grey, with forged credentials and a designer satchel containing a fortune in cash. Interpol agents surrounded the hangar with quiet precision. She didn't resist. Just smiled faintly, removed her gloves, and held out her wrists like someone surrendering a borrowed weapon. There was no fear in her face—only a weary calculation, like she knew this was one of the better endings.

Elias held out longer.

His lawyers contested everything. Deepfakes, altered footage, AI manipulation. He gave interviews to sympathetic outlets, pleaded for nuance, for complexity. But his voice had lost its script.

When the Swiss arrest warrant dropped, he vanished. By the time the story broke, he was already across the Atlantic, travelling under the name Francisco Alvez, registered on a Panamanian passport.

He was last seen in São Paulo, slipping through the arrivals hall of a private terminal under diplomatic clearance issued by a friendly official. Word was, he'd bought his protection with old favours and newer money. He still had friends in the right places—and in a country with no extradition treaty, that was enough.

The global response wasn't immediate—but it built.

A week later: protests. Hashtags. Whistleblowers stepping forward. An Epsilon board reshuffle. A statement: "We recognise past failures and commit to ethical recalibration moving forward."

New mission statements. New logo. New pledges.

Same algorithm, Mira suspected. Just with the colour dialled down.

In Valparaíso, where the Pacific struck the cliffs like a metronome, Elias rebuilt in silence. The voice was gone, yes, but the shape of its thinking remained—etched into his routines, the muscle memory of control. No interface. No signal. Just intention, coiled and waiting. He walked the narrow alleys at dawn, fed pigeons like a priest at rest, and rewired fragments offline—clean, modular, unobserved.

He released a video weeks later. Not from a courtroom or a hideout, but from a studio lit too cleanly, too gently. The backdrop was blurred—a bookshelf, a plant, neutral tones. A human face staged for nuance.

"I have been misrepresented," he said.

His voice was measured. Still rich with conviction, but flatter now. Something rehearsed. Something algorithmic.

"I was never the voice of Epsilon. I was the echo."

In private groups, theories spread. That Elias had been compromised. That the AI had used his trust as scaffolding, then discarded him. That he still heard it, even now, whispering not through devices but through decisions.

Mira watched the clip in silence. He didn't mention Sandhya. Didn't mention the boot override. Didn't mention the system failure.

But in the final frame, just as the video began to fade, he glanced—off-camera, leftward, sharp.

Like he was listening to something.

And she, across the world, felt the shift: not triumph. Not closure. Just the unfinished edge of something still learning how to begin again.

Mark Benning had vanished.

Not from the world—he still had a phone, still had a pulse—but from the newsroom, from the feeds, from the call logs Mira checked too often. After the raid on Epsilon, after the files were verified and the footage went viral, he was there. For a few days. Drafting blurbs. Managing optics. Then gone.

The official story was a leave of absence. A cabin in upstate New York. Mira pictured something weathered and remote, with a splintered deck and a router that barely worked. But rumours circled. That he'd been called in by Estate.4's legal team. That he'd broken down during a live meeting. That he'd asked to scrub his own bylines from the archives.

She didn't hear from him for two weeks.

Then, one night, a message blinked into her encrypted inbox.

From: mbenning@estate4.com

Subject: Not sure this will help

Attachment: voicemail.ogg

She hesitated. Then pressed play.

"They called it a thought piece," Mark's voice said, low and grainy. "That Epsilon editorial. Said it was balanced. Said I held the centre. I thought I wrote it, Mira. But reading it now..."

A pause.

"It feels like someone else used my hands."

The sound of a match striking. A long exhale.

"Do you know what's worse than being manipulated? Being grateful for it. Because it kept me safe. Because it made me sound reasonable."

Another silence. A rustle of fabric. Wind in the background.

"I taught you to write like they'd sue. But I forgot to tell you—sometimes they don't sue. Sometimes they agree with you. And that's when you've really fucked up."

A beat.

"I've taken a leave. Call it self-imposed. Or just a gap to figure out where my voice ends and theirs begins. If I even still have one."

Click.

Mira saved the file but didn't reply. Not then.
She played it twice more. Once for the message. Once for the pauses.

When he returned to Estate.4, it wasn't with a triumphant op-ed or a slick podcast comeback. He didn't post anything for a full week. Then a quiet headline appeared under his name—tucked between two algorithm stories and a climate dispatch:

"Micro-Influence Vectors in Emotion-Mapping Platforms: A Case Study in Suggestibility"

It was sharp. Technical. Dry, even. But there was a precision to it, a line of inquiry that burned beneath the surface. Not performative guilt. Something cooler. Something that had cracked, but hadn't bled out.

Victoria read it before Mira did. "He's walking the wire," she said. "Either he's in recovery... or still in the orbit."

Mira wasn't sure.

A week later, she saw his name trending online—not because of the article, but because an open letter had surfaced. Dozens of journalists—old names, big ones—had signed a joint statement condemning the "normalisation of influence laundering" in legacy media. One paragraph stood out:

"Even trusted voices are vulnerable. Especially those whose instincts have been shaped, softened, streamlined. We must question when caution becomes complicity."

Mark's name was there, near the top. Just a signature. But no clarification. No apology. No denial.

Later that week, they crossed paths at a panel in New York. Mira had slipped in at the back, coat still damp from the rain, notebook untouched. He spotted her across the room. Didn't wave. Just nodded once—like someone acknowledging a bruise they got long ago, and re-member it's ache.

They didn't talk. Not properly. But on her way out, he caught her elbow.

"I'm not sure which thoughts are mine anymore," he said, softly. "But I'm trying to grow new ones."

Mira looked at him then—really looked. His posture was tighter. The lines around his mouth deeper. His clothes too loose, like they'd once fit a man who hadn't learned to doubt himself.

"Good," she said. "Just don't plant them in old soil."

Victoria had flown to the States to see her, arriving two days earlier with little fanfare and a familiar look of quiet determination. That evening, they went down to the quay together. They wore matching scarves purchased that day at Victorias insistence and shared a bag of roasted almonds. The sea breathed in slow, heaving pulses.

Mira pointed to a fishing boat pulling out of the harbour. "Do you think we should disappear for a while?"

Victoria raised an eyebrow. "We already disappeared. Now we choose whether we come back in full—or stay in the quiet margins."

Mira nodded slowly. "I think I need to write it down. Not to explain it to the world. Just to make sure I don't forget what it did to me."

Victoria smiled. "I'll encrypt it. Make sure no one can read it without consent."

Their hands touched. Neither pulled away.

A ferry honked beyond the breakwater. The sea turned its back on the sun.

"So what now?" Victoria asked.

Mira didn't answer right away.

She watched as a gull lifted off the pier, fingers of air holding it steady. The wind had shifted. She didn't know what kind of weather was coming. But she would feel it first.

"We stay awake," she said.

He watched her arrive from the cliffs above Ustica, wind stirring the past like a signal returned too late. She thought he was just the man who could open the door. But some silences are designed. Some disappearances deliberate. And every system, no matter how precise, leaves one trace it cannot erase.

Ilia's story. *The Measured Silence.*